This enchanting, beautifully written fantasy carries us through war, childhood, dysfunctional parenthood, and even love. Wildly inventive and endlessly certain in its uncertainties, *If You Ride A Crooked Trolley* . . . casts a spell and invents a world of true (entirely fictional!) adventure. — JACK FOLEY, poet (*Riverrun)*, critic (*O Powerful Western Star!*), and radio personality ("Cover to Cover")

Unlike many books, this was quick to get off to adventures and the excitement that I was looking for. — MILES, age 12

If You Ride A Crooked Trolley . . . is a pleasure to read — for both children and adults. My son finished the book in one sitting — a rare occurrence! — DAVID GRAYSON, Miles's father is the author of *Discovering Fire: Haiku & Essays* and a frequent reviewer of books on haiku.

We read *If You Ride A Crooked Trolley* . . . last year, and I still remember Petey and Sharlotta, the Korgans and the Paonas. Their exciting adventure sticks with me even after all this time! — JOSEPH, age 14

Thanks for letting me read your story — it was thrilling! — JOANNA, age 14

Reading *If You Ride A Crooked Trolley* . . . was inspiring, especially for the graphic novel I'm working on. — EMILY, age 18

(*Editor's note*: Joanna and Emily are the author's nieces — and so might be slightly biased!)

"Must-not-be-late-for-school, must-not-be-late-for-school, must-not-be- . . ."

Otherwise

If You Ride
A Crooked Trolley...

*A Tale for Children
and Their Adults*

*By Christopher Bernard
Illustrated by Nancy Batra*

A *Caveat Lector* Book

REGENT PRESS
Berkeley, California

Paperback
ISBN 13: 978-1-58790-669-5
ISBN 10: 1-58790-669-4

E-book
ISBN 13 : 1-58790-670-8
ISBN 10: 978-1-58790-670-1

An earlier version of this story, under the title
The Ghost Trolley,
was serialized in the on-line magazine
Synchronized Chaos.

Cover illustrations by Nancy Batra.

Any resemblances between the characters, places, or events
depicted in this novel and any persons living or dead or
actual events or places are purely coincidental.

MANUFACTURED IN THE U.S.A.
Regent Press
Berkeley, California
www.regentpress.net

For Em, Joanna and Sean

Contents

" 'Never imagine yourself not to be otherwise than what it might appear to others that what you were or might have been was not otherwise than what you had been would have appeared to them to be otherwise.'"

"I think I should understand that better," Alice said very politely, "if I had it written down . . . ."

— Lewis Carroll

If You Ride a Crooked Trolley . . .

If you ride a crooked trolley
You may never know the end.
Can you tell me, O Miss Mollie,
Will I ever find a friend? . . .

— Traditional

Chapter 1

A Town and a Boy

The town was called Halloway. More than a century ago it had been a seaside village where fishermen went out each morning for cod and menhaden and lobsters and the streets were full of shrieking children and the sour smells of the harbor. There were mysteries about its past: rumors about an eccentric old woman being burned alive in the town during the Salem witch trials. Another rumor had it that, a generation later, after he was killed in an ambush by the Puritans, the head of a rebellious Indian chieftain was stuck on a pole outside the town's palisade and left there as a warning for any other ambitious young natives.

A pleasanter rumor was that Halloway had been the last stop on the underground railroad for slaves trying to escape to Canada before the Civil War. But like the other rumors, there was no certain evidence to prove it one way or the other.

Then the fishing failed and the town fell on hard times. Businesses closed, much of the younger generation moved out, and the town seemed to burn out, shrinking into itself like a disappointed old man. Over the decades the small harbor silted up.

Then the war struck. Even this remote place was traumatized for four long years, tragic telegrams coming to the small community, until, like a gigantic Roman candle, the war, just like the town had before, burnt out. However, once the war was over, the town started flickering again: young couples living in the big cities were eager to forget the war's privations, and, like many another quaint seaside place, the town was rediscovered — or maybe it would be truer to say it had been discovered only now — and for a time it became a highly fashionable resort for the summer, with a trolley service and new streets planned and sewer lines and new telephone posts riding out far into the surrounding countryside like threads from an enterprising spider's web.

But those times were ever a roller-coaster ride: the state was hit by another economic slump, the summer trade petered out, and the town was once again forgotten, apparently burnt out for good. The hotels shut down, unfinished houses crumbled away with no one to occupy them, and to top it off, the local pastor murdered his wife and ran away with the church funds. The new roads ended in the middle of the surrounding woods, and the sewer lines stayed hollow and waterless, empty and echoey to the young local boys who stuck in their heads to try the acoustics with a mighty shout and explore their mysterious labyrinth.

Halloway had finally been almost forgotten when elderly New Englanders discovered the forlorn little town near the sea, filled with untouched architecture going back half a dozen generations: a sweet little place, they thought, to retire to (the darker historical rumors suppressed by the local chamber of commerce, which collectively held its breath as it saw new inhabitants and businesses slowly trickle back into town). One of the retirees, a mailman from Burlington, Vermont, posted on the internet photographs of Halloway in its quaint autumn splendor, though locals knew the deepest beauty in the region always came in the dark heart of winter, when the sun disappeared like molten bronze through the stark, leafless woodlands.

A computer worker in far away California saw the photographs and promised himself to visit the lovely town next time he was back east. And when he did, he found himself not only in a pocket of natural loveliness, but also in an oasis in time, where people kept up old "analog" traditions on the verge of vanishing from the rest of the twenty-first century — scrimshaw, sampler weaving, knitting bees, building matchstick sailboats inside old whiskey bottles, writing the entire U.S. Constitution on a kernel of dry yellow corn . . .

Then the Great Pandemic hit, and he and anybody in the world who could was forced to work at home. "And that means we can work anywhere we can live," he had said to his wife, a twinkle in his eye. It didn't take much coaxing to get her to agree to move to the picture-postcard-perfect town that very summer from their cramped condo in Palo Alto, the mortgage for which had eaten half their salaries.

Their friends in high tech soon learned how happy the young family (power coder, brilliant spouse, rambunctious daughter, and a Huskey) seemed to be, and how perfect the peace and quiet, far away from the punishingly high housing costs where they were still trying, pandemic or not, to make a living. And, naturally, they became envious . . . So, over the next year or so, late into the night, the dark streets became increasingly lit by prim New England house windows behind which diligent techies worked, coding, testing, recoding, retesting, sending ghostly communications all over the world from this place which could be anywhere and so, in a sense, was nowhere.

Halloway had an Episcopal church with a white spire pointing heavenward and a small library with statues of John and Abigail Adams out front. Regularly you could hear, in the distance, the clang-clang of one of the trolleys from the service built long ago during the resort's glory days.

Oaks and maple trees and sycamores lined the streets. Once, a deer, long thought to have abandoned the area for the inland hills, was seen standing in the early morning on the local notary's lawn, sniffing the dawn air as if listening to a far-off call.

One day near the end of the years of pandemic that wrapped the globe in their unforgiving grip, of wildfires turning western skies shades of crimson and suffocating the air underneath, of a near civil war provoked by leaders gone nearly berserk after turbulent elections, a young computer game programmer and his wife (who sold fashions on the internet and had a passion for Russian writers) decided to make the move they had been considering for years, between "putting out fires" domestic and professional or as they drifted exhausted off to sleep each night, with a hope, seemingly ever more fanciful, yet therefore all the more necessary: to escape, somehow, some way, to a far-away, hidden place of quiet, peace and safety in a world where everyone seemed to be going mad at the same time..

As experienced "techies," neither of the couple

was tethered to an office, so they had taken a deep breath and decided to move away from the "tent city for billionaires" (as the ironic young woman called San Francisco, where they had been sharing an apartment with six other techies for an egregiously high rent — and where "never in the next millennium" would they be able to buy a home). But where to go? Then they had seen the idyllic little New England town and its many pictures on Instagram.

It offered an ideal combination of rustic seclusion and the stimulation and conveniences of the digital age — Netflix, Amazon, social media, even Zoom chats for those starved for those wild, anything-goes, "business" meetings. ("Not," snorted the programmer.) They would be able to live and work comfortably while paying off their astronomical student loans. It appealed to the earnest romantics in them. And Ms. Stephenson (she was old-fashioned enough to have taken her husband's name, but still insisted on the "Ms.") had family in a city an hour or so away, Aunt Marguerite, the aging doyenne of her eastern relatives. Above all, it would be far away from "the mad, mad, mad, mad world."

Halloway, once they moved there, seemed everything they had hoped for — or as much of "everything" as they knew they could reasonably expect. They loved the snowy season and the hot and lushly verdant summertime (though it was not too hot by the edge of the gray Atlantic; and it was a novelty for them to watch the sun rise above the ocean after all their lives seeing it set into the sea, and another novelty to see a world of green and rain after living through endless summers of desiccated tans; the very light seemed saturated with deep blues and greens they had never seen before, and the long, deep twilights were hauntingly beautiful), and they loved the colorful motley of the forests in the fall, and the unexpected surge of bliss that each spring brought them after the white, piercingly cold winter.

The move brought another pleasant surprise. A year after they moved, they had a child (it made so much more sense to start a family in their new home), and the Stephensons named him Peter Myshkin, after the hero of a famous Russian novel and one of Ms. Stephenson's favorites.

He was a curious little boy — in both senses of the term (as his great Aunt Marguerite noted on one of her visits from the city a hundred miles to the south): an "oddity of a creecha," full of wonder at this peculiar planet he had fallen to as if from outer space, full of doubt at people's glib responses to his questions about why things were done the curious way they were here, full of objections to many things that seemed to strike many people as reasonable but struck him as ridiculous, and full of what he considered stupendously great ideas, a number of which, rather notoriously, backfired, such as his invention of a self-administering bathtub for their cat Max, or the self-propelling slingshot that turned rather too quickly into a boomerang and almost knocked the inventor's eye out, or his revenge on Chace Fusillade, the son of their wealthy neighbor, for Chace's burning of Petey's homework assignment about the Civil War hero Harriet Tubman, which paradoxically made Chace one of Petey's best friends but made their parents enemies for life.

"Is Peter a *complete idiot*? The boy is impossible!" his mother lamented to his father, adding accusingly, "And where did he get that orange hair? We're all blond in our family!"

The father — a quick, irritable man with a beard as thick as a hedgerow, and who looked older than his years, though he generally acted decades younger — would roll his eyes, twist his lips and say nothing, or smirk to himself, which made his witty, willowy wife hopping mad when she caught him. (His attitude was, leave the unanswerable alone. There was no *conceivable* app that could do it!)

But the mother could never leave unanswerable questions alone. And soon they would be in the middle of one of their rows, which were becoming harsher over the years, as they blamed each other for their unhappiness in the old town far from the mad world they had tried to escape but had brought with them like an invisible horde of monkeys on their back, a horde that despite all the gifts of Halloway, had only grown with time once they had gotten over their honeymoon with the town.

The Stephensons, it seems, still believed in happiness, and they blamed each other for not finding it. Sometimes they each had the same sad thought, but one they were too afraid to share with each other: perhaps they had expected too much from Halloway, and Halloway, through no fault of its own, had let them down.

Petey, alone in his room, exploring something in his home-made lab — the wing of a late summer moth, a crystal of purple mineral he had found in the garden, the mysterious result of mixing unknown chemicals in his little glass retort — would overhear these exchanges, which would build in intensity until the whole house seemed to shake with their fury (even when that fury was silent as the grave), and then, feeling frightened and ashamed, the young boy would sneak to a distant corner of the house where he didn't have to know what was happening.

That place was often the bathroom, and he would look at himself, with alarm and scorn, in the mirror. What he saw was a moonlike, pudgy face, with two questioning brows above blinky eyes and a pug nose covered with freckles and a small chin and two large, shapeless ears.

Was he stupid? Was he ugly?

The mirror stared back at him silently. "Well, what do *you* think?" it seemed to ask.

So: was it maybe true that it was *entirely his fault* that his parents fought all the time like two mad dogs in a back alley?

Maybe he really was an idiot. They valued above all things cleverness, good grades, cunning. His father made a big deal about outsmarting his rivals in the company, which he claimed he could do even three thousand miles away from the hothouses of Silicon Valley, and both parents loved to play verbal one-upmanship games, sparring over dinner until his father, who was always a little behind his mother in the quick, blunt verbal rejoinders department, grew red in the face.

Petey's grades in school were not bad. But then everybody's grades were not bad. Even a true, genuine dope (*everybody* agreed on this one) like Charley Dunkin didn't get really bad grades — just not bad *enough*.

On the other hand, if Petey truly *were* an idiot, how would he possibly even know it? This was a conundrum that gave him much food for thought until his brain ached.

And then there was the other question: why was his face so round? Neither his mother nor his father had a round face. Even his grandparents had high cheekbones and long faces, like horses.

And where had his orange hair come from? He used to be quite proud of it, it was unique, no one else he knew had orange hair (except a long-forgotten politician his parents sometimes brought up instead of the bogeyman, to make him go to sleep at night) — but now he *hated* it.

And he hated himself. The mirror didn't lie: he was fat, and he was ugly, and he was stupid . . .

He had been a mistake. He was sure of it. (The other day he had overheard Kelly in homeroom whispering to Melissa that Gretchen had been a *mistake*. No wonder nobody liked Gretchen, Kelly had whispered! Even her parents *had never wanted her*!)

The more he thought about it, the more convinced he became. It explained everything. Why had he been born so soon after they arrived in Halloway? Had they perhaps moved here so they could hide him from their families, so they would never even know he existed? He had never even seen his grandparents, except on Skype, and he sometimes darkly suspected they were actually CGI . . .

He grew quieter around the house, and started saving his pestering questions for his teachers at school, and his reveries for the privacy of his room at the end of the corridor off the dining room, where he had a bed and a desk and a bookcase and his stuffed toys (Andy, Lionel, Monkey, and Lucile) and his telescope and chemistry set and his laptop and his charger, and a window that overlooked the backyard with the swing set and a great casement of sky speckled and sandy with stars on a cloudless winter night for as far as the eye could see (like last night, after the snow stopped and the moon rose like a face – round like his own – brooding over a stark world white and glittering), and a door he could shut, turning his room into a place where he could dream up entire universes, inventing any possibility, worlds on worlds, far from all perplexities and shame . . .

Chapter 2

The Trolley To

As the trolley clanked around the corner in the freezing predawn, Petey noticed how it looked kinda funny. With its single headlight glaring like the head in the raised hand of the headless horseman, it lumbered with a determined squealing straight toward the little boy where he'd been waiting, alone and half-frozen, under the old, flickering streetlight.

But Petey had never seen this trolley before, battered and leaning perilously over like it had just a drop too much at its last stop and moving toward him unsteadily through the early morning fog.

The bell clanged twice, and the curiously vulnerable-looking machine groaned as it rolled down the rails. There was no other traffic on the icy streets, and the night was pitch dark beyond the cones of light from lamps disappearing in the fog up and down Buckingham Street.

The trolleys he rode each day to and from school were blue and green, but this one was painted a dirty yellow, and a route number and destination the nine-year-old had never seen before appeared above the windshield in glowing capitals: "2 OTHERWISE."

What a weird name! It must be someplace out near the ocean, or far in the other direction, where the old unfinished roads died out and the woods began. Someday he'd ride to the end of the line, maybe with his buddy Chace Fusillade, and they could find out what and where this "Otherwise" was. But right now he had to get to school, "Pronto!" as Daddy said.

He hugged himself, his breath steaming in a shapeless white cloud in front of his face, and frowned ruefully. He'd been waiting here for almost half an hour. Why was it so late? He mustn't be late for school — not today!

The front end of the trolley, like that of most of them, looked like a face that was trying to hide a joke and doing a bad job of it.

Petey jumped in and clambered up the steps as soon as the trolley stopped. He asked the driver, who he could barely see where he sat in the dark cabin, whether this trolley went past his school.

"Yes, young man," said the driver's voice. "It does."

Not entirely convinced, Petey slipped a school token into the coin box, trudged to a seat near the back and sat himself down.

The trolley, strangely, was empty, so, feeling a little odd and out of place (there would usually be at least half a dozen of his schoolmates inside, some still half-asleep, others joking or already bickering), he sat down half way to the back, where he usually did if he could, and stared hard out the window, careful to watch and see if the trolley turned off on one of the branch lines that would take him in the wrong direction so he could get off fast.

He had been late far too often of late, so much he'd been threatened with suspension if it ever happened again.

It was unfair; it wasn't as though he was lazy. He'd had good reasons for being late. Once it had been because his mother had overslept after a particularly nasty late night quarrel with Daddy. Another time it had been because he'd had to make his own breakfast and prepare his own lunch. And the last time it had been because the cat had run away after the failed bathing invention and he'd gone looking for it. It took days for Max to come home again, nosing his way back into the kitchen one evening with an offended air. He never seemed to quite trust Petey again, no matter how much the boy petted and told him he was sorry.

Now school was threatening Petey with suspension. He'd been suspended once, for breaking the principal's window with a paintball gun while playing with Chace. It had been an accident, he hadn't meant it. But his father had beaten his bottom with a broken surge protector when he got home that night, shouting at him to "apologize! Apologize! Otherwise I'll . . . !" And maybe for that very reason, he had clammed up.

When he was grown up, he'd run away. Then they'd be sorry! . . .

He listened to the trolley as it moved over the rails, seeming to say, in endless repetition, "Apo-lo-gize, oth-er-wise, apo-lo-gize, oth-er-wise . . . " and stared sleepily up at the winter sky.

It was a blue so dark it was almost black above the snowy ground, with the stars going out one after another like distant candles in a huge cathedral (he had been inside a cathedral once, in New York City, it had been so impressive when the sound of the organ had suddenly burst in waves of music across the immense shadowy nave!), and there was a pasty pallor in the eastern sky just above the horizon where the sun would soon be rising, and he felt his eyelids grow heavier and heavier as the trolley clanked in a lulling rhythm on the tracks. The sky just before dawn always seemed to be beckoning . . . "Must-not-be-late-for-school, must-not-be-late-for-school," the tracks seemed now to be saying, over and over, "must-not-be-. . ."

He felt his eyes becoming heavier and heavier. Whatever he did . . . he must not . . . miss . . . his school . . . stop . . .

Soon he was fast asleep.

"Otherwise!" the trolley driver suddenly called out. "Last stop!"

Petey started awake — *Oh no!* — and rushed to the open door.

He halted.

If he got out now, how long would it take him to get the next trolley back?

On the other hand, if he just stayed on this trolley, it would have to go back eventually — wouldn't it?

He looked around him. There was nobody in the trolley car but himself and the driver.

Suddenly the door closed.

Overcome with despair, the boy returned and plopped back down in his seat and stared into the blackness outside, imagining the principal's face twisted in wrath as she suspended him and the reaction of his angry and "disappointed" (that awful word saved for only the most unforgivable humiliations) parents.

After a small torturous eternity that was in fact only ten minutes as the driver took his break (Petey could hear him grumbling to himself and slurping his coffee, or whatever), the trolley suddenly jolted awake and started moving again.

But something strange happened: instead of turning around, it continued going straight ahead.

The boy felt a little spike of panic, craning his neck toward the driver, though all he could see was the tall back of the seat inside the little cabin, and a jacket swinging from side to side on a hook near the front door. Then he turned back to the window and the darkness outside. He would never make it to school on time.

Then something happened to him. Oddly, now that there was nothing whatever he could do about being late for school (the sound of the trolley's wheels on the track seemed to say, over and over again, "nothing-you-can-do-about-it, nothing-you-can-do-about-it"), the despair collapsed over him like a great wave and immediately washed away, leaving behind it a strange tingling feeling — a curious combination of helplessness and a feeling of resignation, a sense of irresponsibility, and a peculiar feeling that he recognized, after a moment, was — *yes!* — relief.

He even felt a little thrill.

What would happen next?

Where were they going?

What would he find there, in this place with the strange name "Otherwise"?

And the yellow trolley carried him ahead into the darkness.

Chapter 3

A Girl in a Red Jacket Under a Green Sky

As the trolley clanked noisily down the tracks, it suddenly emerged from what looked like a tunnel, but no — it was an old covered bridge, of the kind seen in the woods near Halloway, and that Petey always thought looked "romantic," like his mother said, to a guffaw from his father — even eerie and haunted, though in a way that wasn't scary. He had always liked the bridges, with their rumbling, uneven planks as the family car slowed down to drive across them with long shadowy interiors dotted with sunlight peering through cracks and the smell of damp, decaying wood. But this one wasn't rumbling at all. Nor was there any sign of sunlight.

For the sun was only just now rising through the trees ahead of the trolley.

But Petey noticed something strange. It made his heart skip a beat. The shadows on the other side of the bridge looked all wrong: rather than falling from right to left across the trolley rails, which they should be doing, the shadows now fell *from left to right.* The trolley had been running north, unless they had made a weird turn when he was asleep. But that was impossible; they would have been back in Halloway by now if that had happened, not in the woods at all. If they were still in the forest, they had to be north of the town. And they were definitely in the forest.

At that moment the trolley moved across a break in the trees — a meadow cut through by a racing stream — before moving back into the darkness.

And above the meadow was the sun. And it was blinding him.

Petey had to throw his hand over his eyes. This was crazy — not that he had to cover his eyes against the sun, but because he shouldn't have had to do that in the first place: the sun shouldn't have been on that side of the trolley It was in *the wrong position.* It was rising *in the west, not the east.* Petey pushed close to the window and looked up, past the blazing patch where the sun silently roared.

The sun was rising into a sky without a single cloud across its vast and shining expanse.

And the sky was pale green.

And not only that: it wasn't winter anymore.

Petey pinched himself. Yep, he was awake all right, unless you could pinch yourself in a dream and still stay asleep.

There was no ice or snow anywhere, not on the ground or in the trees or in the crevices of the trolley's windows. The banks along the trolley tracks were covered with a thick blanket of ferns, brush, wild flowers — a blossoming tapestry with a complicated blend of fragrances so strong and lovely he pressed his nose against the window crack so he could smell it better. It looked like, and smelled like, a drowsy, dewy morning in late spring. He pushed the window open as wide as he could.

Not only was the sky green, but some of the vegetation — the long grasses, for example, and some of the weeds — was *blue*. He could see clover (also blue) on the banks of the trolley cutting, and, on a sudden zephyr, several blew through the open window into the trolley. He picked one up from the seat next to him; it was a four-leaf clover! At first he felt "hella lucky," as his dad would say, then he picked up two others that had blown in beside it: they were all four-leaf clovers! For some reason, this made him shudder.

He peered more closely at the forest the trolley was passing through. It also was different: the trees had pale gray bark, as he was used to seeing, but the boughs didn't start till high up, leaving the lower trunks smooth and bare, and the roots started several feet above the ground, forming little, cozy cage-like shelters at the base of each tree. And the leaves looked strange: each tree had leaves with many different shapes, some of them like the wings of birds, others like seashells, others like palm fronds or banana tree leaves, some like oak or maple or sycamore leaves — but they were all on the same tree, which was definitely not how he knew trees grew back home.

Back home! But if this wasn't "back home," where in McGillicuddy's bean patch (another favorite "dad phrase") was he?

He heard what he thought was birdsong, as it was coming from the trees, but it wasn't like anything he'd ever heard: there were long sharp hisses, then chattering and ratchety crackles, followed by a little, spiky shrieks. And then he saw the little furry animals that were making the noises; they were flying through the trees, though they were definitely not birds!

They sailed through the treetops like flying squirrels, though these looked more like chipmunks, one of them like a possum, another like a rat, another like a bright red fox; they spread their arms, the skin spreading out from their torsos like little sails or wings as they flew from bough to bough. There was even a monkey or two hanging out in the upper branches, but quite tall and with less fur, and they stopped and watched the trolley intently and seemed to notice Petey and watch him with an especially alert look on their wizened faces. The forest looked like a jungle!

Petey tried to crouch out of sight when he saw the monkeys watching him, though he was immediately mad at himself: so what if the monkeys saw him, let 'em look! He had nothing to fear from them — did he?

Other mysterious eyes were watching him from the dense foliage of the trees: large round eyes in small round heads, bracketed by curiously stirring wings. One pair of wings took off heavily to follow him as he rode past, followed by another, then another, and another . . .

Not long afterward, the trolley came to the edge of the forest. At first the brightness of the sun dazzled the boy and Petey held his hand above his eyes like a hat brim until he could focus again. The first thing he saw clearly was something lying on the ground near the tracks just ahead of the trolley.

It looked like the body of a man. He seemed to be sleeping. He lay with his face in the grass, with one arm stretched forward as though he were trying to hold on to something that was no longer there. Maybe it was one of the homeless people Petey sometimes saw in Halloway, usually from one of the big cities not far away — Portland or

Burlington. Petey felt a spasm of pity for the man as his body passed beneath him and to the rear.

The boy, his eyes fully adjusted to the stark morning light, suddenly looked at the landscape surrounding him.

It was partly hidden by what looked like brown fog, that blew away here and there to reveal patches of blackened, in some cases still burning houses, barns, sheds, stables, granaries, silos, whole farmsteads, charred woods, fields pocked with craters like holes punched out by a crazed giant; and villages were burning in the distance. The waves of smoke moved across the land like ghosts.

The boy was at first too astonished to be frightened. It looked too awful to be real, and he felt at first a certain detachment, as though none of this was happening to him; it was like being thrust without warning into someone else's nightmare.

A solitary bird was winging slowly above a dead tree. But it was flying upside down.

Then the boy saw something that made him shiver: the driver's seat had changed — before, it had been on the left-hand side of the trolley, as it always was; but now it was on the right. He still couldn't see any sign of the driver: just the tall back of his seat, and his coat, now on a hook on the other side of the driver's cabin, swinging back and forth. The mirror above the driver's head, in which he could usually see the driver's face, was blank.

The bell clanged three times, and the trolley moved onward. Petey squeezed his face against the window and stared as they moved across the desolate landscape. What had happened? Why had he heard nothing about it? Something like this would surely have been broadcast on the news — wouldn't it? What was this? Where was he?

Then he saw her. It was a little girl dressed in a red coat, though the coat was covered with black streaks like stains; she was standing in a field next to the trolley tracks, watching the trolley come toward her. She started waving frantically.

The trolley stopped and she got in, mechanically put a coin into the coin box, and walked back with head down toward Petey as the trolley moved forward. Petey watched her intently as she sat in the seat across from him without apparently noticing him.

She was a small girl, with frizzy hair and honey-brown eyes, from what he could see; her skin was smooth and brown, like cocoa; like the skin of Sambene, the little African American girl in the other fourth grade class, who Petey had a crush on but had never told anyone.

The girl heaved a sigh. Her cheeks were stained with tears and ashes.

Petey wasn't sure what to do. His parents had always warned him against talking to strangers. But, under the circumstances, wouldn't it have been terribly rude to say nothing at all?

"Hel-lo," he said shyly, his voice breaking between the syllables.

"Oh, hallo!" the girl said in a small, startled voice, seeming to notice him for the first time. She turned toward him; yes, her eyes were as brown as honey.

Petey's heart skipped a beat, for the second time that morning.

"What happened out there?" he asked, after hesitating for almost a full minute.

The girl stared at him with large, sad eyes that hardly seemed to see him. They shone with tears.

"They come for us!" she said, in a curious accent Petey had never heard before.

"Who came for you?"

"The Korgan of Ramora! It part of the big battle last night. You must see that!" And bursting forth from having been pent up so long, her words came tumbling out. "They come in middle of night and take me father and me mother and me sister and me brother, and they take me if I not hid under bush at back of our garden, and they set our house on fire, and I have to wait all night, watch our house burn down, and I ken't believe it so I look at it when it all over, and I slip and fall in the ash, then I run away as sun rise till I see the yellow trolley that cross the middle of Otherwise when there be a blue moon, like there be last night, and here I am . . . "

Petey tried to take all this in, without quite succeeding.

"Why did they want to take you?"

"It part of the war . . ." The girl looked at Petey closely for the first time. "Don't you know? Not you from here?"

Petey shrugged uncomfortably.

"No, this is the first time I've ever been here. I got in the trolley to go to school and I fell asleep and I missed my stop and I waited for the trolley to take me back but it took me here instead."

"Oh," said the young girl, still sadly. "That must mean you from Howtiz."

Petey, who had never heard of "Howtiz," looked doubtful, but felt it would be impolite to contradict someone who looked so upset.

"This be Otherwise," said the girl, wiping the tears from her eyes (telling her story seemed to have relieved her a little). "You can see the different destination on front of trolley. When it go back from here it say '2 Howtiz.' In Otherwise, things be different from Howtiz, completely different, but not all at once, which why it called Otherwise.

Anyway that what me deddy tell me. I only know Otherwise, I never be to Howtiz. I always want to go there, because Otherwise not exist without Howtiz — at least that what me deddy tell me some of our philosopher say, though other philosopher claim otherwise. Me deddy say that so like them. They never make up their mind about anything."

Petey blinked at that. Philosophers claimed otherwise about Otherwise? The thought gave him a little brain spasm.

"Anyway, I always want to see for meself, by going there on yellow trolley. But me parents never let me go. And a blue moon be rare anyway." She sighed again. Speaking clearly made her feel calmer, so she continued. "We live, I guess not anymore, in Forest of Paal. Me deddy a teacher. Me mummy a doctor, and there be three children. We live peaceful before the war and the Korgan from Kingdom of Ramora across Mountain of Sleeping Noor invade we. Everyone force to join one side or other, either Korgan or Paona, who be largest group who live on the plain. It easy for we to choose, cause Paonas gentle and honest, but very poor, and there not be many of them, and Korgan, though they be rich and powerful and strong, and there be many of them, not content with what they have but think they must have ever'thing. They probably not even be content then!" she sighed

31

The girl paused, as if uncertain whether to tell the boy from Howtiz any more.

"You couldn't just stay out of the fight between them?"

"No," said the girl positively. "You do that, everyone turn on you. 'Whoever not enemy of me enemy, be enemy of me.'" She said the last in a detached singsong voice, as though reciting a school lesson she had become profoundly and bitterly skeptical of.

Petey looked uncertainly at the girl. He was thinking about what he saw altogether too often on the news back home. Back home! Sigh . . .

"Are you sure we are in Otherwise?"

"Yes, of course! Why you ask such a question!"

"Because what you say sounds an awful lot like where I come from."

"The world Korgan and Paona fight for not just world of Otherwise," she continued, ignoring Petey's remark, "it be world of Howtiz, too. Whoever win will take over Howtiz as well. The two world come together then into one world — for better or worse. At least so some of our philosopher say . . ."

"When they aren't saying otherwise?"

"Exactly right!" She gave a little laugh. "I doubt anyone know, really. But that what me parents tell me."

The boy felt rather solemn after he heard all of this.

The girl looked straight at the boy.

"But," she said, leaning in toward him; seeming finally to make up her mind to tell him everything, "there be another reason Korgan invade."

She stared hard at him with her honey-brown eyes.

"They invade to find Spell."

Petey gave her a blank look.

"So, what is 'Spell'?"

"Spell be secret of Otherwise. Or one secret," she added conscientiously.

The two children looked gravely at each other as the trolley moved quietly onward. The sun was just behind the young girl's hair, making it glow.

"Me deddy tell me the story. Spell discovered many generation ago by the Paona. At first it make them happy, because it give them power over whole world, me deddy tell me. But it soon come clear such power can also destroy world, and so it too dangerous to keep. It too much for Paona to know. And so they bury it in a distant, hidden place and try to forget it. But my father say fact they once have that power can never be forgotten, never utterly entirely. Every so often someone break down and try, in middle of night, because it against law and every commandment of our religion, to dig up Spell, but no one ever able to find out where it buried.

"Then one day me deddy, who also like to invent things — mostly toys for childers, but sometime big important things for adults — thought he had worked out — completely by accident, he say, but I think he just modest — what Spell be. Last night he tell me mummy. And I overhear them." The girl's face looked almost frightened. "I not sure I hear everything, but I remember everything he say."

"But what was this 'spell' all about?" asked Petey impatiently. "Why was it so dangerous somebody would start a war because of it?"

"First of all, you must know Otherwise only exist because different things happen in all kind of different ways, but by chance," said the girl. "Anyway, that be what me deddy say though I don't really understand it. What Spell do be this: it make possible to go back into past and change into future — What Be. Even more: *What Is.* That why it be so powerful. It possible for you — for anybody — to make another Otherwise, and then another, and then another . . ."

Petey stared at her.

"If you have Spell, you have power over all of time. And therefore over all of world. So."

And the possibilities this suggested to him

swirled through Petey's mind in a flash of intox-
icating wonder.

Chapter 4

The Exploding Trolley

"What be your name?" the girl asked politely.

"Petey," said Petey, coming back from his momentary trance.

"Me name be Sharlotta."

For some reason Petey blushed, and the girl lapsed into silence. She seemed a good deal less upset now.

"Our home so beautiful," the girl said quietly as she stared across the ruined landscape outside the trolley windows. "It not big, like a gookor, it be more like a gimpy, but it be roomy enough, and cozy. We live there long as I remember. Me mummy say I born there, but I think that can't be so. After all, my little sister born in a gorpal in town." She was silent for a moment, then continued dreamily, "We have two kerdles, and we have a bumble who think he a kerdle, and we have a goffney out back where we grow cispies and prunables and gerk trees that unleave in the fall and flourish all winter until the kerries turn many colors in sprang, and we have a wintry house where we eat when it not rain, above a custer with a pearly so fresh and cold you can kneel at the bank and cup your hands and drink it whenever you thirsty, it be most delicious beverage in the world, me deddy say." She stopped, as though the dream had abruptly ended, and her face again crumpled. "Now it all gone . . ."

Petey had hardly understood a thing that Sharlotta had said, but her words sounded so heartfelt he too felt deeply sorry that it was gone, and he sighed.

It was then he heard an angry series of shouts from in front of the trolley, which came to an abrupt halt. The two youngsters were thrown from their seats to the trolley floor.

Petey scrambled up and peered around his seat toward the invisible driver. The jacket had fallen from the hook.

Sharlotta stayed down behind the seat in front of her.

"It be *them*!" she whispered in a terrified voice.

The trolley's back door, which was right in front of them, had been thrown open when the trolley halted. Petey took the girl's hand and, without a word, they scurried down to an embankment thick with tall ferns and other brush, and hunkered down among them out of sight.

Two large males, dressed like soldiers from a bygone era and holding weapons that looked to

Petey like a weird blend of crossbow and machine gun, their skin as pale as milk but looking like they hadn't washed in months, walked up to the trolley's front door, looked inside and waited.

The driver didn't emerge. Petey, who had never gotten a good look at the driver, was curious to see more, but Sharlotta tugged his sleeve to keep down.

Petey could hear the Korgans talking in the distance, but could neither see them nor make out what they were saying.

"Maybe we should get away from the trolley," he whispered uneasily.

They crept up the bank to a cluster of curious-looking trees at the top — their canopies of leaves were broad at the bottom and narrow above, twisting up in a shape like a flame. From there Petey could see clearly into the driver's cabin: there was no one in the driver's seat! His father had said that driverless trolleys and busses were only a matter of time — but he had never seen one before.

In front of the trolley several Korgans were conferring. Then one of them walked to the trolley's open front door and threw something inside. The Korgans then ran hell bent for leather for cover behind a stand of tree fifty feet away.

"Hold your ears!" Petey had just enough to say when there was a flash, a rush of air and a boom as the trolley exploded.

Dust and gravel and shattered fragments of metal and glass, shreds of plastic, rubber, straps, handles, fixtures, stuffing from the seats, bits of wire, lights, piping — all rained down as the two children sat with their hands over their ears. Papers and fragments from Petey's backpack and the things inside it scattered in the air suffused with the smell of burnt gasoline and oil.

They sat paralyzed as the noise from the explosion echoed away in the distance.

How will I get home now! Petey thought. His backpack and notebooks and homework and lunchbox, and — gee whillickers! — his new smartphone, his very first one, which sure would have been useful to have right now — were all gone in a blast of smoke and noise that made his ears ring.

After a moment, Sharlotta brushed away a large piece of plastic seating that had fallen lightly on top of her, and whispered to Petey, "If them I follow, them me lead to me family."

Petey didn't need to ask who she meant by "them."

"Aren't you scared they'll catch you?"

"Of course I be. But how else I find them?"

The girl raised herself a little.

"Are you going by yourself?" Petey asked.

"Yes. Unless you want with me come."

"You know, it's too bad you're wearing a red jacket," he said, after a moment, still in a whisper. "They'll see you a mile away. Like," he added, shyly, "my hair." Fortunately, he was wearing a little, dark blue watch cap, as it was still winter in Howtiz; his orange hair peeped through in a narrow halo around the edge.

Sharlotta nodded ruefully.

She couldn't just take her jacket off. She had only a thin nightie on underneath.

"But if you wear it inside out . . ." Petey said.

The girl's face brightened. Then she whispered, "Don't look!" took off the red jacket, turned it inside out, and put it back on. The lining was a blue-green and would blend in with the landscape quite satisfactorily, at least from a distance.

"There!" said Sharlotta. "Now you can look."

"Who talking up there?" called out a voice from below.

They heard sounds of climbing and took the plastic seat cover Sharlotta had brushed aside and, curling up together into a little ball, covered themselves up.

A pair of muddy boots moved through the grass toward Petey, stopping a few inches from his nose.

There was silence except for the sound of the wind and the shrieks of flying animals in the trees.

"Strong smell of Paona!" The voice came from behind Petey's head; it took a deep breath. "Some find it repulsive, but I find it likes me. I smell it can here."

Petey felt something touch the seat covering himself and Sharlotta. It felt as if one of the Korgans had raised his foot and was resting it casually on the seat.

"Humph. No doubt explosion scaring them off."

The voice above the boots spoke. "I need interrogate the leader Laghdin dragged in last night. I have word he knows more than he has a right to. Laghdin found paper before they burned house that tells he may have it. Or part of."

"Hm! That be a lucky find indeed!"

"Or not . . . "

"It mean quick end to war," the other said, almost ruefully.

"Or not! We keep it to ourselves till we have more fun with Paonas. Why spoil the game when our boys just start to enjoy themselves?"

"Ah, now you thinking like true Korgan!" said the other.

And the two laughed and ambled away down the embankment.

"He be talking about me deddy!" whispered the girl.

Petey met Sharlotta's eyes in the shadow of the cover.

"Well," said the boy, "I guess we'll have to follow them now."

He saw in the shadows a complicated look on the girl's face: a knotting together of fear and sorrow and determination and gratefulness.

They quietly pushed the plastic off and peeped above the grass. A half-dozen Korgans were walking down alongside the trolley tracks, their strange weapons cocked over their shoulders. Petey and Sharlotta followed at a distance, through the trees above the tracks.

"One thing I don't get," said Petey quietly. "You said your family joined the Paonas, but the Korgans said your father is a 'big shot.'"

"We not Paona," said Sharlotta, "we be Creel, related to Paona going back many a generation. Me deddy become a Paona leader after we join them in the war, so they consider him Paona too. They consider anyone who join the Paona Paona. It just one more way they be coarse and stupid."

"And the Paonas don't do that?"

"No, of course not. They not lump everybody together the way Korgan do. Everyone be different, be treated differently. Anyway, that what Paona believe. And we Creel believe that too. But we should not talk. The wind blowing from us to them. They might hear."

The two children followed the Korgans until the latter walked past the tracks, down a twisting stream, then turned out of the woods to the edge of a wide plain. Petey gasped a little at what he saw: an immense encampment going for miles and made up almost entirely of tentlike structures, spread across the landscape like a living quilt, swarming with thousands of living beings — "Korgans," said Sharlotta to Petey's unasked question.

Pocked with open spaces, parade grounds and sturdier constructions of wood and even stone, and divided up by a network of roads and pathways, and surrounded by a belt of fencing punctuated with bannered towers, it was the main camp, as Sharlotta explained to Petey, of the invading Korgans. Far in the distance, a range of mountains crowned with snow seemed to float above the horizon in the image of a sleeping woman, and a blue moon hung in the eastern sky.

"That," said Sharlotta, gesturing toward the mountains, "be land of Korgans. From there they come to conquer us, to seize Spell, and conquer world."

Chapter 5

One Eye

The two children crept up to a fallen tree just a stone's throw from a gate where the Korgans had entered. Soldiers were beginning to come and go, carrying burdens of various kinds, nondescript bags and crates, some of them weapons — what looked to Petey like spears and rifles combined in some weird way — and a few civilians, servants of the military, on early morning errands and chores outside the camp. A burly guard kept watch, eyeing his fellow soldiers with deep suspicion as if expecting at any moment to find a spy.

The Korgan with the muddy boots had glanced back as he entered the gate with a salute to the guard, who stiffened to attention. Petey noticed muddy boots had only one eye. The other was covered with a patch.

Sharlotta whispered, "We got to get into camp somehow — "

A strange, cruel shriek interrupted her. Under a tree nearby a trio of scruffy-looking Korgan kids — a few years younger than the two — were playing, to the two children's horror, a cruel game

44

of toss-the-kitty. The kitten mewed frantically, its little tail spinning as it flew as the little Korgans tossed it back and forth with yips and shrieks of a mean pleasure. A large tabby sat crouched in the grass, its tail fluffed, its mouth open and clicking ominously, its eyes watching the kitten being tossed back and forth with a look of fascinated hopelessness.

"So terrible!" whispered Sharlotta.

Petey scowled under his watch cap. He always hated seeing helpless creatures being tormented.

A moment later Sharlotta said, "Where you go?"

"Just a sec." Petey slipped away into the brush.

A few minutes later a stone came flying out at the Korgans. Then a second. Then a third.

"Paonas!" shrieked one of the little Korgans.

The kitten fell onto a soft patch of grass and the three kids ran off, disappearing through the gate. The guard ignored them as he peered hard at a passing soldier hunched under a box of projectiles. "Ain't you seen me a thousand times, Harree? Watcha staring a' mee loik ya' thought me were a Paonee?"

"Maybe ya' bee, Jorok!" snarled the guard. "Ya wouldna bee the feerst t've turned tween dawn 'n' noon on a visit outer the gates."

The guard's brief distraction did not go

unnoticed: Petey ran from the brush, swept up the frightened kitten, and ran back with it to Sharlotta.

"Mew!" went the kitty. "Mew!'

"Poor thing!" Sharlotta whispered, cuddling it against her cheek. "You safe now."

But the kitten didn't look too sure of that.

After a moment, the large tabby emerged from a bush and sat nearby, staring at them suspiciously.

"Must be the mom," said Petey. Sharlotta placed the kitten carefully near the tabby, who hissed instinctively at the young Creel, then sniffed at the kitten, bit it by the scruff of the neck and carried it swiftly into the brush.

"Now all we must do be to get into camp," said Sharlotta.

"And follow One Eye."

Suddenly they looked at each other. They had gotten the same idea.

"We have to dress like Korgan children," said Petey.

It was a little trickier than that, of course: they would have to disguise themselves until they con-vincingly *looked* like Korgan children.

"Well," said Petey, in a subdued voice, "their hair is dark, and really long . . ." His own hair was bright orange and very short.

"And dirty! And full of snarls!" Sharlotta's voice was filled with disgust. "And clothes of them be all muddy, and they look they have not had bath in one month!"

Petey looked solemn: he did not exactly enjoy taking baths himself, and in fact had skipped one last night, so he could get up early (anyway, that had been his excuse). He hoped Sharlotta hadn't noticed.

"But that means," he said, "that if we get all dirty, and rough up our clothes and hair, they might not notice we're not Korgans. After all, adults never really look too closely at children who aren't their own."

"Yes," Sharlotta said thoughtfully, "I notice that."

"And if they do look, and think we don't look quite right," Petey said, brightly, "they'll just blame their parents!"

So, not having a better idea, and needing to get into the camp as soon as possible so they could follow One Eye, they set about roughing up their hair and clothes and smearing mud on their faces and hands, and making themselves look generally scruffy and grungy and beat-up and dirty. Petey had to apply a lot of mud makeup to the hair at the edge of his cap: it took a lot of dirt to hide the orange, even when he pulled the cap down to his ears.

"There be one good thing," Sharlotta said cheer-fully. "I can wear my jacket right side out now."

Now the smears of ash stains looked just right for a scruffy Korgan girl.

"How I look?" asked Sharlotta after they were done.

Petey looked her over doubtfully.

"Your hair looks too pretty."

Sharlotta scowled.

"And your head look too ugly! You never have to comb long hair full of snarls!"

"And it's way too clean . . ."

Petey, without further ado, filled both hands with mud and splattered it over Sharlotta's hair, at the same time grabbing and violently matting it.

Sharlotta shrieked.

"What you doing! Stop that! Right now!"

They started wrestling and fell in the mud.

"What's goin' on over there?" a Korgan voice rang out.

A shadow fell over them and they stopped, suddenly terrified.

Petey glanced up and saw, against the sun, the guard with his lance staring down at them.

"Quit fightin' and get back into camp. There be Paonas around here, and they eat little-uns like you for breakfast. Go home!"

The children, covered with mud and with their

tangled, dirty hair in their faces, were too frightened to say a word, so they stood up and scampered through the open gate into the camp.

Chapter 6

The Camp of the Korgans

The children were faced with a spaghetti of dirt lanes and passages through which a strange assortment of ox and donkey carts and curious-looking tanks, with long snaking treads, snout-like guns, and tall, needle-like turrets, and fat, tubby armored cars and troops of Korgans moved, mostly armed soldiers, some marching in platoons as their sergeants barked orders, some on the backs of horse-like creatures, or on patrol, some bustling about on unknown errands, some sitting in front of their tents, cleaning their weapons and trading jests.

Among the crowds were more civilians, women and children and a few old men and women, but all of the Korgans looked curiously fierce, whether because of the styles of the clothes they wore, or their habit of expression, or just how they were born; they all looked angry about some unknown grievance, and Petey quickly decided he had better put on his "angry face" if he hoped to fit in — even though he didn't feel especially angry, just excited and a little scared — and looking scared he realized would definitely not do.

The camp was as big as a small town construct-ed entirely of tents and cabins, huts and sheds, armaments depots, bivouacs, lookout towers and long, ramshackle barracks above which flagpoles rose and the Korgan flag flapped loosely in the morning air — a black flag with a pair of lightning bolts crossed inside a crimson circle.

The children had no time to investigate their surroundings and didn't want to stand out by gawking, so they scampered down several lanes till they found an unused tent in a vacant corner and crouched behind it. They had been right: no one had paid any heed to them; they were just a pair of urchins playing in the street.

One curious thing that Petey noticed about the Korgans: though the hair of some of them was brighter and shinier than that of others (they ran from sandy to streaked, from dark to dirty to plati-num, and some were even like what Petey's moth-er referred to contemptuously as "peroxide"), they were all, every single one of them, blond.

"You know what?" Petey suddenly grinned. He felt quite exhilarated.

"What?"

"That was fun!"

Boy, Sharlotta looked funny, with her hair all mussed and full of mud! But maybe he should keep the thought to himself. Girls could react weirdly to teasing — not like boys, who would just push you and tease you back, then forget about it.

Petey was also going to tell her about making sure she put on her angry face, like the Korgans, but she looked angry enough on her own, now they were in the camp, so maybe she didn't need to be told.

Sharlotta looked askance at Petey.

"There must be special place where they keep prisoners," she said in a whisper.

"I'll bet he'll take us to it if we can find One Eye," said the boy. "He was talking about having to interrogate your family."

"That was the other one. But no matter."

"It was One Eye."

"It was the other one!"

"No, it was One Eye! And anyway, we only know what *he* looks like."

Sharlotta was silent, with dignity.

"All right, Know-It-All, and how do we find him?"

Petey stared down at the dirt between his knees where he was crouching.

"Well, stay here we cannot," said Sharlotta. "They will not come to us. How do I look?"

"Honest?"

"Honest."

"Terrible!"

"You sure?"

"I'm sure. You look terrible!"

"Good," Sharlotta said stiffly,

"How about me?"

"Well, you look *awful*!"

"You sure?"

"Of course I be sure!"

"Really truly awful?'

"Really truly *awful*!"

"Good!"

Petey rather liked the idea of looking awful but decided not to press his luck by asking a third time.

He paused and took a breath.

"Are you ready?"

"No. But that not matter, yes?"

Petey shrugged.

They both took a breath, and went out into the camp.

There was a feeling of increased tension in the air. Korgans on duty seemed especially busy, rushed, and even off-duty Korgans looked tense; a truck bristling with armed soldiers careened through the street past the two children, the soldiers shouting pedestrians out of the way.

Many of the soldiers had covered their faces

with red and black war paint, and their solid, hard bodies made the ground rumble as they marched past on the double.

Soldiers walking the streets greeted each other with sharp, animal-like cries.

Some of the Korgans looked at the two children a little too closely, a cold gleam in their eyes. Petey was especially worried Sharlotta didn't look quite "terrible" enough. Maybe she was one of those girls who, no matter what they did to themselves, always looked nice. He should have put more mud in her hair.

He was going to tell her to cover her face with her bangs when a Korgan suddenly stopped them.

"Hey, girlie!" he said, grinning at Sharlotta and pulling her hair away from her face. "Anybody tell you you cute as a Paona? Bet you get that from fellas all the time!"

Sharlotta stared furiously at him.

"And you," she shouted, "look just like a Korgan!"

The Korgan hooted, laughing, as the children scampered off.

Sharlotta pulled her hair over her face until only one eye peered out as if through a parted curtain, without her companion having to advise it.

They huddled behind a pile of junked weapons, watching the passing parade. Drums thundered, trumpets rang out, and cries of "Ramora, Ramo-ra!" and "Death to Steed!" echoed through the camp as a war party gathered in a parade ground in front of them.

Then, from a broad space between two low barracks, a solemn procession emerged and moved toward them.

Chapter 7

Bang Bang and Blue Moon

Columns of armed soldiers in black uniforms and helmets, with the strange crossbow machine guns across their chests, marched in precise and mechanical order, their simultaneous tread shaking the ground. Behind the soldiers moved a platform, like the floats Petey had seen in parades at home, but draped in red and black, on which stood a Korgan, in a commanding pose and wearing scarlet robes and a black cone-shaped hat, like a wizard at a Halloween party, that Petey would have laughed at any other time. He looked to the young boy like a priest and held a staff shaped like a young dead tree, its branches writhing in profile against the sky. Behind him rose a monumental figure of crossed lighting, like the figure in the banners, but all of gold. The priest's face was covered with red streaks like war paint. And kneeling in front of him, two acolytes held up an open book as he made elaborate gestures with his small, gloved hands and chanted in an incomprehensible tongue.

The platform, a kind of large moving altar, was

being pulled by a mass of tall, delicate-looking creatures, with pointed ears and elven features, and patches of fur on their cheeks and arms, heads and faces, and they dragged the platform with long ropes tied around their shoulders and waists. They seemed vaguely familiar to Petey. Two Korgans with whips "encouraged" them, with shouts and lashes, to keep moving in time with the marching soldiers.

Suddenly the boy realized where he had seen them before, or creatures like them. They were like the monkeys he had seen when the yellow trolley had first entered the forest in Otherwise.

"That must be Altar of Ramora," Sharlotta whispered. "I hear of it but never see it before. And those are Paona. Prisoners that have been turned into slaves."

Petey realized something else that was strange and unsettling: if the Paonas were like *monkeys*, then the Korgans *were like people* . . .

Behind the altar a choir of Korgans in black robes solemnly marched, singing a hymn to the rhythm of the marching soldiers — but it was like no hymn Petey had never heard in any church he knew.

It was a series of blood-curdling cries and swooping yells, with fists raised to heaven, to discordant blasts of trumpets and drums.

Behind the angry choristers came a crowd of Korgan women, looking cowed and fearful, their hands clasped before them and their heads bowed. And behind the women scampered a rag-tag gang of Korgan children, whooping and shrieking.

Sharlotta and Petey watched as the procession passed. Then a couple of the Korgan children following the women ran up to them. One of them picked up a pistol from the pile of junked weapons and started waving it.

"Bang, bang, Paona!" he shouted at Petey. "You dead!"

"I'm not a Paona!" Petey shouted back, immediately regretting it. Being silent would probably have been wiser just now; this was not the first time that thought had occurred to him, invariably a fraction of a second too late.

"Yes you be!"

Petey glared back at the boy.

"You new here?" the girl Korgan asked Sharlotta, in a deep, froggy voice.

"Yes," Sharlotta said, carefully lowering her voice to imitate the other's frogginess.

The boy aimed his pistol at Petey.

"Bang, bang! You dead!"

"Where you from?" asked the girl Korgan.

"Over there." Sharlotta pointed vaguely toward the east.

"The land of the blue moon?" the girl said, sounding skeptical. And the blue moon was indeed already drooping in that part of the sky.

"I said you dead! Now fall down!"

Petey glared even harder at the boy. He would not fall down just because he was ordered to.

"I always wanted to go to the land of the blue moon," said the girl.

"You fall down! You dead! I just kill you!"

"Maybe I can come and visit you?" she asked politely.

"If you want," said Sharlotta in her froggiest voice.

"No, *you* fall dead!" said Petey, who pulled a pistol out from the pile and started waving it at the boy.

There was the sound of a little explosion. All of the children stared in alarm at the Korgan boy: his pistol had gone off, the bullet just missing Petey's head.

The hair on the Korgan boy's head rose like the fur on a frightened cat, and he threw down the pistol and ran off, followed by the girl, after a shrug and a shy glance back at Sharlotta. "Boys!" she cried out as she ran off.

Petey dropped the pistol and the two of them ran behind the pile as a massive Korgan soldier picked up the fallen gun and tossed it onto the pile.

It was One Eye.

"You!" he shouted.

Petey felt a hand grab his shoulder and lift him bodily from the ground.

This is it, thought Petey. *I'll never get home alive.*

"Many times you be told to play never around weapon dumps." The Korgan spoke in a calm, measured voice, like a more brutal version of Petey's dad's. "How often tell you we must? You might kill someone. You might kill each other. You might kill *me*."

One Eye gave Petey a single fierce shake that made the boy's teeth rattle (unlike his dad, who rarely did more than give him lectures and send him to bed without his smartphone), then opened his hand and let him drop to the ground.

"Now go home. And take your friend girl with you." One Eye looked at Sharlotta, whom he had not even bothered to chastise — she wasn't sure which insulted her more, this, his calling her Petey's "friend girl" or his general attitude of condescension and contempt. She was about to give him a piece of her mind when Petey — seeing her turn red and open her mouth — pulled her away, and they ran off, as ordered. Sharlotta glared back, with fury in her eye, and caught One Eye staring after them strangely, with his lone, inflamed iris, as though he had noticed something that did not seem quite right. Then Sharlotta noticed that Petey had a tear in his cap, and a patch of his hair was exposed, like the bright skin of an orange.

They ran behind a horse cart and stopped.

"Some of your hair be showing through a tear in your cap," said Sharlotta.

"Oh!" said Petey. Unfortunately, there was no mud where they were, but there was some dust, which he applied vigorously. "How does that look?"

"A little to left — no, to right — no, to left — no — yes — here, let *me* . . ."

And Sharlotta applied her hands to his head as Petey scowled.

"There," she said, "that better, anyway. What be your parents thinking when they give you orange hair?"

But Petey had no time for another tedious debate on that subject.

"Look!"

One Eye was walking away after commanding a guard to keep watch over the weapons pile. Petey pulled the young Creel to the other side of the cart as One Eye disappeared into a warren of lanes among a chaos of tents, then they followed, at safe distance, after him.

One thing made it easy for them: the black

strip of his eye patch stuck out against his dirty yellow hair, even in a crowd of Korgan backs, so they didn't have to follow too closely. Sharlotta was worried he had seen through their disguise, but knew there wasn't much they could do about it. As long as they didn't bump into their new Korgan "friends," Blue Moon and Bang Bang.

They threaded slowly through the colorful encampment, passing whole mini-villages where tangles of Korgan families lived, with smells of cooking by the small Korgan women wafting across them (and making both of them hungry, as Petey hadn't had much breakfast, and Sharlotta hadn't eaten since before the raid on her home the night before) — smells of baking bread and soup and coffee — with long lines of washing hanging out to dry, showing the array of Korgan fashions for men and women, girls and boys, and even their undergarments waving like banners in the breeze (Petey was left wondering at some of those, they were so peculiarly shaped, whereas Sharlotta delicately pretended not to notice) — but all the time keeping One Eye in sight, losing him only once, when he turned into a weirdly constructed little hut with a chimney three stories tall and didn't come out for ten minutes, and they thought they had lost him for good; then he came out, adjusted his belt and continued on. Petey turned to the young girl and grinned. "A Korgan outhouse!"

At last One Eye turned into what looked like a litter dump in a distant corner of the camp where skinny, famished pariah dogs lurked, biting and snarling at each other over snatches of left-over garbage. He approached a forbidding-looking tent, black and low. Two guards at the entrance saluted him sharply, and One Eye saluted cursorily and disappeared inside.

The sun stood, brilliant and hot, at the peak of the green sky.

Then a light wind began blowing.

Chapter 8

The Black Tent

A dozen yards from the tent stood a rock outcropping shaped like a perched falcon, and the children crouched behind it and watched.

Then they heard the sound. At first it was soft, almost gentle, something between a sigh and a groan; except that it seemed to go on too long. Then it slowly became louder, until it was almost a low, deep wail, going on and on, on and on, until suddenly it burst into a ferocious yell, followed by a sound of deep sobbing, and then the words "No . . . ! No . . . No . . . " The words turned into a whimper and finally trailed off into silence.

Sharlotta suddenly curled up against Petey's side.

The sounds started again.

Tears appeared on the young girl's cheeks as the sound again grew again to a climax before again fading away.

"Me deddy," she said in a small, trembly voice, and her little arms hugged Petey.

Petey awkwardly put his arm around the girl's shoulders.

They sat there for a long time, holding each other as they listened, but no more sound came from the tent.

Then something caught the corner of Petey's eye and he looked over Sharlotta's shoulder.

It was stepping carefully through the trash and garbage, making its way past the snarling dogs, which yipped at it and made it stop briefly and hiss and growl before stepping carefully ahead again. It didn't seem to notice the children, even when it passed near them, but continued on toward the black tent as though with a definite destination. Petey watched it casually walk past the guards to a corner of the tent far behind the entrance. Then, glancing back as if directly at Petey, she stuck her nose inside a tear in the tent wall and slipped inside.

It was a large tabby cat. Petey thought it looked awfully like the large tabby whose kitten they had saved from the Korgan kids — maybe it was the same one?

There was a gleam in the cat's eye just before it slipped into the tent.

"I have an idea!" Petey whispered.

"Oh?" said the girl, miserably — it was not the first time she had heard those words — as Petey snuck away.

Sharlotta was beginning to wonder where the

boy from Howtiz had gone when a shout erupted from one of the guards as a cloud of smoke brewed up from a trash pile nearby on the other side of the tent, and the guards ran to stamp it out.

A few moments later she nearly jumped when she heard someone run up behind her and turned around, with a flinch. Petey stood near her with an uncontrollable grin; flashing a half-used-up book of matches with a picture of Jackie Robinson on the cover that he always kept with him as a lucky charm.

"Wait!"

"What?" Sharlotta's whisper came from just behind his left ear.

"Don't push!"

"Why not?"

"Because there's a big hole and I don't want to fall in."

"But me foot be sticking out! Maybe they see me!"

"I can't go forward or I'll fall into the hole!"

The darkness enfolded the two children like a blanket of untouchable velvet.

They had just poked inside the tent where the cat had gone, the torn flap just big enough to accommodate them.

Petey's eyes had not yet adjusted to the dark.

He had stopped because his outstretched hand was dangling over a void, groping for a floor that wasn't there.

They had to wait what felt like an agonizingly long time before their eyes adjusted to the darkness. They could hear the guards busy stamping out the fire and too distracted to notice the kids sneak under the tent wall.

Slowly out of the darkness the two eyes of the large tabby appeared, looking at them from where it sat perched not far away. What was wrong with these peculiar animals? it seemed to think. Couldn't they see in the dark? At least they'd had sense enough to follow her into the tent.

Petey saw a shadowy light rising from below, then the outlines of a deep pit at the bottom of which he and Sharlotta could have broken their necks if they had fallen in.

Except for the sounds from the frantic guards outside, there was dead silence in the tent, and a cold smell of damp earth penetrated the air.

"There be steps," Sharlotta whispered, her eyes adjusting quicker than Petey's. "Down the hole."

Petey made out a set of rough wooden steps winding down the sides of the pit to its distant bottom.

The tabby blinked, then started nonchalantly washing its face.

Petey crawled over to the top of the steps, with Sharlotta, who was finally able to pull her exposed foot into the tent, close behind. Then they cautiously descended, only once making the wood creak loud enough to waken whatever slithering creatures inhabited the pit.

The bottom of the steps led to a short corridor lit by a burning lamp sputtering in the gloom. A rusty iron door stood at the other end. From behind the door came an eerie stillness, especially after what they had heard outside the tent. Then the door creaked and started to open.

The steps were openwork and gave little cover, but the children had no choice but to scurry under them as quietly as they were able.

One Eye came out with an irritated look — the sounds of the guards fighting the fire could still be heard coming from above — then he closed the door and walked up the stairs, his dirty boots passing within inches of Petey's face: the same boots he had seen on the embankment.

The children hunkered down.

"He not lock the door," the girl whispered.

As soon as the steps stopped shaking from the Korgan's tread, the two children scurried out and down the corridor, then pushed against the door, which opened silently.

The boy sucked in his breath.

Chapter 9

The Secret of the Tent

Lined up along one wall of the small, airless room, tied and gagged in a squat on the dirt floor, were a very young boy, a little girl toddler, and an even younger girl and a young adult woman, all with the same soft, cocoa-colored skin as Sharlotta's.

They looked up tensely at Petey as soon as he came in, as though expecting only the worst: Petey realized he must look like a dwarf Korgan. But when Sharlotta came in behind him, pulling her matted, muddy hair from her face, their faces widened with a shock of joy, and they began giddily trying to talk through their gags. The look on Sharlotta's face when she saw them was even more startling: she looked like she wanted to shriek with happiness, but was doing everything she could to keep silent, and the result was that her face flushed a deep purple.

But Sharlotta's joy turned into something more terrible when she saw, in the far corner of the room, tied to a chair under the room's only light, a middle-aged man with torn clothes and a bruised face and a cut above his left eye, blood trickling down a gray-streaked, bearded chin. His right leg was twisted in an unnatural way. An empty stool stood in front. The man looked up at them, with a look in his eyes of defiance and fear. Then an incredulous smile flickered to his lips as, through his daze, he recognized his eldest daughter.

"Deddy!' Sharlotta cried out despite herself.

"Sharlee . . ." her father murmured, and fainted.

"Quick, quick!"

But Sharlotta was already busily untying the ropes binding her father. Petey soon untied and ungagged the others, telling them to keep silent, while Sharlotta, after undoing the knots, tried to revive her father by hugging and coaxing him and whispering in his ear. He had woken but was groggy and weak. He could barely walk (one leg was almost dislocated) and could only stand with the support of his wife, who, in terror and exhaustion, seemed to feel she had no choice but to look to Petey and her daughter for guidance.

"We be blindfolded when they bring us here," the mother said, "before they begin . . ." She couldn't use the word "torture" ". . . on your father. No knowledge have I where we be."

"We be in black tent in trash dump in Korgan camp on Quixiona Plain at edge of Avana Forest," said Sharlotta. (*So that's where we are*, thought Petey. He had been wondering, though the information was not entirely enlightening.)

"But how you be here?"

"Too much to explain!" said Petey. "We gotta get out of here before One Eye gets back."

They didn't need to ask who he meant by that name.

Seeing the ropes used to tie up Sharlotta's family, lying on the floor like sleeping snakes, had prompted a thought in Petey, which he whispered to Sharlotta and her family. They agreed it was their only hope of escaping.

Petey took the longest of the ropes — the one that had tied up Sharlotta's father — and carried it with him into the corridor.

"I be coming with you," said Sharlotta in a hush, following him on tip-toe.

"Okay," whispered Petey. "Close the door."

"Why?" said Sharlotta.

"It's got to be dark."

"But what about . . ." and she pointed toward the corridor lamp hanging above their heads.

"Just *close* it!"

Sharlotta scowled; she didn't like being ordered around, especially by a boy, but, since this was his idea, and so far his ideas had worked, she complied and closed the door.

Petey swung the rope up toward the sputtering lamp and, after a few swings, managed to extinguish it. The hall went pitch black. Then they groped their way to the winding steps and quickly ascended toward the half-light penetrating the tent till they were nearly at the top steps.

"Good enough," a voice said outside the tent above them. "You be able to handle the rest." It was One Eye.

Petey tied one end of the rope to a post at the side of the steps, then stretched it across, a few inches above the step, tying the other end to the opposite post. Then he did the same thing across the next step down. The two children snuck down and hid under the steps at the bottom.

They had just gotten there when they heard someone take a step on the wooden stairs above them: one step, then a second, then a third, regular and heavy, making the wood creak slightly.

Petey felt a seizure of panic. Had the rope come undone?

Suddenly there was a curse and a cry, followed immediately by a clattering thundering and the steps clattered and swayed as though about to collapse over the heads of the children, and a body came tumbling to the bottom and along the ground several feet in front of them in the pitch dark, then gave out a long groan and sigh, and was still.

Sharlotta whispered after a moment of silence, "He be dead?"

"I don't know. I don't think we should find out."

They gingerly tip-toed through the dark, feeling for the Korgan and sneaking around the big outstretched body, which was shuddering and wheezing (*Not yet!* thought Petey as he squeezed past), then they opened the door to the cell. Petey looked back at the unconscious Korgan. He looked like a sleeping giant that might wake at any moment. His single eye was open and stared crimsonly at him.

"It work!" said Sharlotta.

The eyes of her own family shone in the light of the room's little lamp, and Petey opened the door wider and showed them One Eye outstretched on the floor.

Petey led them out and around the unconscious Korgan, then up the steps, slowly, as the father was unable to move fast; Petey untying the ropes when he got to them and giving them to Sharlotta, who tossed them into the darkness below, like dead serpents dropping down a well.

There was only one way out of the black tent now, Petey realized, as Sharlotta and her frightened family sat on the topmost steps near the flap where he and Sharlotta had entered. He took his little book of matches with Jackie Robinson on the cover and went over to the side of the tent furthest from the flap.

There was only one match left.

Then Petey heard a distant groan, coming from the bottom of the pit.

He was recovering. If he found them, they'd be worse than dead.

The boy hastily struck the last match — a little too hastily. The tip sparked and sputtered, and almost went out (the matchbook had gotten wet from the mud), till he moved his finger down so the rest of the match could catch fire, by so doing almost burning himself.

Then, biting his tongue hard so he wouldn't cry out as the flame bit the end of his fingers, he knelt and touched the flame to the bottom edge of the tent wall where it almost touched the ground; he hoped the canvas was not wet.

Please burn, tent! thought Petey, biting his tongue as hard as he could. *Nice tent! Come on! Please! Burn!*

He was about to either drop the match or shout out with pain when the canvas slowly began to respond.

It was a very small and very weak flame, and Petey, afraid it would die before it had half a chance, took out his handkerchief and fed it, like

kindling, to the little crescent of red eating its way
a little at a time up the black canvas.

Then, suddenly, the fire took.

Chapter 10

Escape

He ran back to the torn flap and cautiously looked outside.

"Fire!" cried one of the guards, as smoke began billowing from the back of the tent. Both guards ran toward the new fire.

Almost simultaneously a shout came up from the bottom of the steps.

Petey pulled Sharlotta out by the hand, who pulled her father, who pulled her mother, who pulled her little brother, who pulled her little sister, and out of the tent they slipped, the father hobbling painfully, over to the rock outcropping in the shape of a falcon a dozen yards from the black tent. The tent was rapidly being eaten by the flames.

The wind had grown in force, whipping from the north.

A flame shot up behind the tent, like a great yellow and red tongue, with the sound of low, muffled boom. In the distance Korgans turned with startled looks and after a moment began running toward the tent.

The escapees ran as fast as they were able (the mother helping the father hobble along at a pace that was agonizingly fast for him), weaving through piles of debris, past wreckage and heaps of cast-off equipment and slurries of blasted rock, to the far side of the dump and a half-collapsed wall along the edge of it, a hundred yards from the fire. As they stopped and were huddling down in the narrow shadow of the wall (the sun was high and hot), Petey slipped and fell on his face. The ground where they were standing was thick with mud.

Sharlotta stared at Petey as he picked himself back up, blushing from his clumsiness through the new layer of mud on his face, then said excitedly to her family, "Do like we do!"

And she started speading mud over her brother and sister's faces and clothing.

"It be our disguise."

"Of course!" said her mother, with a flash of pride in her clever daughter.

The father weakly began applying mud to his face. "I doubt I ever be able make this ugly mug look like a Korgan," he said. "No matter how hard I try."

"We see about that," said the mother, who began vigorously spreading mud over his head and hair where he couldn't see. Her husband returned the favor, smoothing mud over his wife's pretty, cocoa-butter face. It was curious to Petey to see the two adults, enthusiastically smearing dirt all over each other — the contrary of anything his own parents had ever commanded of him.

"You know, this be fun," the father said, with a pained chuckle, "if we be in less of a pickle."

Soon they were daubed all over with mud, with wild-looking eyes and dirty clothes and faces half-hidden under tangled and ratty hair.

"There," said Sharlotta, looking everyone over critically.

It was unfortunate her parents stood out so much, by their height and spareness: there was no way they could be disguised as Korgan children, who were, of course, short and almost all squat. But there was nothing to be done about it: they only hoped the adults could be made to look like sick and ailing Korgans, keep their heads down, and take their chances. The mud would hopefully hide the beautiful chocolate brown of their skins.

Petey, now something of a masterpiece of filthy slovenliness, was about to speak when something struck the back of his head.

"Ow!" he cried as he spun around indignantly.

The two Korgan children they had met earlier stood a few yards away, Bang Bang laughing tauntingly and pointing at Petey. Blue Moon stood, giggling, at his side. What were they doing there? Had they been following them? There was no time to figure that out! The two of them began singing out in childhood's universal cadence of mockery:

"You — are — Pao — nas! You — are — Pao — nas!"

Petey picked up a handful of gravel and threw it at them, and they laughingly side-stepped it and started throwing rocks back in rhythm to their chant, which was soon returned in kind, and the rock and mud throwing was in full spate.

Beely, Sharlotta's little brother, grandly smeared from head to foot, began wailing when a pebble struck his nose.

The two parents realized any attempt to stop the fight was likely to call attention to them, so they huddled against the wall and waited for the contest between the children to be resolved.

"You — are — Pao — nas! You — . . . !"

Sharlotta interrupted them, shrieking back in her loudest voice:

"YOU arrrr Paonas!"

Petey picked it up, yelling, with Sharlotta, "You — arrrr — Pao — nas! You — arrrrr — Pao — nas! You — arrrrr — Pao — nas!"

Soon, Sharlotta, Petey, Beely, who, at four, felt he was almost grown up, and Sharlotta's sister, little Johja — who, only three, had no idea what they were shouting — were all chanting together, "You — arrrr — Pao — nas!" outshouting Bang Bang and Blue Moon, and (all except for little Johja, whose attempts at rock throwing got no further than her shadow) assailing them with a crescendo of gravel and handfuls of mud, until Bang Bang was struck on the top of his head by a small rock from the hand of Sharlotta.

He yelled, shocked he was not invulnerable, then started bawling at the top of his lungs. This was the sign for the others to launch an all-out attack, swooping in a stampede. Blue Moon yanked at the blubbering Bang Bang, and they dashed off, the sounds of the boy's bawling floating back on the wind.

"Let's follow them!" Petey called to Sharlotta in triumph — a little too soon, in Sharlotta's estimation. How like a boy! But Petey went on excitedly, "We'll be safe! The Korgans are worried about putting out the fire, they'll just think we're a bunch of kids playing chase!"

("I be no *kid*!" protested Beely.)

" . . . and Bang Bang and Blue Moon might lead us to an exit from the camp! Anyway, we can't stay here." Looking at Sharlotta: "Can we?"

"But what about me parents?" said Sharlotta, looking at them in their resplendent muddiness, her mother holding her father, who was still weak from the terrible things that had been done to him in the tent.

"I can come back for them as soon as we know how we can get out of here."

"He be right, Sharlee," said her father. "It better than all us stay here. But best you hurry. I no like the look of that fire. You go with them, Meena."

"Faar, I no can leave you here," said the mother.

The fire was growing on the far side of the dump despite efforts by the Korgans to put it out. Shouts echoed across the camp.

"We can't wait!" said Petey. "Come on!" And he dashed off after the two Korgan children as they disappeared into a confused crowd that seemed uncertain how to respond to the fire.

"Go! Hurry!" said Sharlotta's mother. "Take Beely and little Johja with you. No one notice four dirty kids running away from a fire. We be all right here."

"Maybe not all right, exactly, but at least we up against a wall," the father said mordantly.

Beely and little Johja looked at Sharlotta with mouths agape.

"Do everything your sister say," the mother said to them in her firmest Mom "don't-even-think-of-talking-back-to-me" tone. "You follow her."

And Sharlotta grabbed their hands and ran after Petey, who had already vanished among the Korgans.

The fire was spreading; they could hear shouts and cries of increasing alarm.

Then there was a big explosion to the north; a cloud of dust swept over them and the shock wave threw them to the ground.

Sharlotta immediately rose, coughing, and looked back to make sure her parents were all right.

"*Go!*" ordered her mother, her arms covering her husband as the dust blew over them. "Go!"

And Sharlotta, hesitant to leave, watching her parents disappear in the dust, finally turned and ran with the little ones in the direction where Petey had gone.

Chapter 11

The Altar of Ramora

But Petey was nowhere to be seen, and they ran blindly on.

Petey had gone off like a shot after the Korgan kids, just managing to keep them in sight as he caromed through the crowds, mostly of soldiers, but also of women and children, civilians and elderly, horses with six legs and donkeys with three ears and odd-looking draft animals he had never seen before: something that looked like a cross between a camel and a giraffe, moving ponderously under a pile of domestic furniture, including a strange kind of piano with a tuba stuck to its back and a stove as long as a sofa, and other creatures, apparently used in battle: one looked like an ostrich covered with armor and with the head of rhinoceros, and another one looked like a flattened hippo with the head of a pig and the beak of a crocodile; it carried a kind of Gatling gun with barrels spread in a circle, slowly twisting like a pinwheel on its side — a strange weapon made to kill everything in a 360 degree circle, leaving alive only the gunner and the piggy hippo crocodile to tell the tale: all of these were either the results of manipulating genes (he had heard about that in school) or different evolutionary paths taken in this weird world called Otherwise, just as the Creels' strange speech was no doubt the result of a different evolution of language.

But he had no time to wonder about these things. Smoke wafted across the camp like an army of ghosts, burning his eyes. He looked back once or twice, looking for Sharlotta and the others. Maybe this had been a bad idea. But it was too late to turn back, and he ran ahead, afraid to lose Bang Bang and Blue Moon in the confusion.

But they were nowhere to be seen.

They had run in the direction of a distant iron-like skeleton of a tower toward the south; maybe that was where he should be going. But first he had to find Sharlotta and her brother and sister.

Then he saw the strange religious thing he and Sharlotta had seen moving through the camp earlier. The Altar of Ramora (as Sharlotta had called it), stood silent and still, draped in black and red, with the crossed lightning bolts rising above the gathering smoke like a gleaming symbol of a dreaded power. Standing in front of a huge tent with spire-like towers, crowned with the forked lightning, at each end, like an enormous temporary temple or church, it loomed ahead of Petey unguarded in the melee, left there after the completion of the macabre ceremony they had witnessed, like an abandoned float at the end of a parade, and he ran toward it.

The bottom of the altar was surrounded by a kind of apron drape, and Petey slipped under it and huddled there, pulling up the drape to peer out at the turmoil unfolding outside.

After a few moments of watching, he slipped out and called, at the top of his lungs, "Shar-lotta!" then scurried back under the altar.

In all the turmoil, no one seemed to notice what must have sounded like a name that sounded very suspiciously un-Korgan-like name — especially given the suspicious fire.

After a moment, Petey slipped outside again and repeated the call: "Shar-lot-ta!" then ran back under the altar. Then he did it again. . . .

Sharlotta and Beely and little Johja were running at random through the smoke and confusion, hunkering down briefly, here behind a tent, there behind a truck, there behind a parked soldier convoy driven in to combat the fire and control the panic. Bursts of crackling gunfire in the near distance made her blood freeze, and her little siblings started whimpering.

This brought unwanted attention, as some of

the adults, mostly female, turned to them with disapproving looks or the kinds of concern Sharlotta knew was the last thing they needed.

They almost ran into an elderly Korgan lady, who turned to them with a worried look on her wizened face.

"You be lost, dear?" she asked.

Beely looked like he was about to offer a candid reply, but Sharlotta wasn't about to let it be known by this woman — no matter how kindly she seemed — just how lost they were, and ran off, pulling the little ones with her.

She wasn't looking where she was going and this time ran right into someone and fell, taking the little ones down with her. Their whimpering erupted into full-throated wailing. Sharlotta, frightened, looked up at the person she had bumped into.

It was Blue Moon, staring down at her with a triumphant grin.

"I knew you were Paonas!" she crowed, in her deep, froggy voice. "Did you set the fire? I bet you set the fire!"

"Quiet now!" Sharlotta shouted at her brother and sister, who were wailing even louder. "We not start a fire! We nearly burn alive ourselves! Look me jacket!" And she showed Blue Moon the black ashes smeared across the bright red cloth, ashes from her burned-down home. "Would I burn my-self? And" — gesturing toward her wailing siblings — "would I bring two crybaby along with me if I mean to start a fire?"

This stopped Beely in mid-wail.

("I be not a cry — !" he was starting to say when he was interrupted.)

"Maybe," said Blue Moon, skeptically, ignor-ing Beely and staring straight into Sharlotta's eyes, "and maybe not. But I think I'll call a guard to find out!"

And she raised her hand to her mouth to call out.

"Do not, please!" Sharlotta pleaded. "You be right — we not Paonas, but we Creels, their friends. We be . . . we be kidnapped!"

Blue Moon snorted. They didn't look very kid-napped. "Who kidnapped you?" she demanded.

"A soldier with eye-patch."

This had an immediate, and peculiar, effect on Blue Moon, whose face went slack, her eyes turn-ing strangely cold as they seemed to penetrate into Sharlotta's own.

A moment passed, and Sharlotta was afraid she had just said exactly the wrong thing.

"You kidnapped by . . . Orgun Ramora?" Blue Moon asked, with the coldness of an adult, though her voice hesitated before speaking the name, as though reluctant to let its syllables cross her lips.

"I not know his name. We just call him One Eye."

"He belong to the royal family." Blue Moon stopped, to let this sink in. "He is the cruelest Ramora of them all. Everyone hates him. Everyone hates . . . Orgun Ramora of Ramora, for his cruelty, for his lies, for his greed, for his cowardice, his arrogance, for his . . ." Blue Moon faltered. Her eyes darkened with a rage that frightened Sharlotta and made the two young ones freeze. "And you . . . you . . . ," she continued, ". . . *escaped him*?"

"Well," said Sharlotta, "we not escape yet."

Blue Moon stared at the three of them. Her eyes suddenly filled with a mixture of anguish and an almost icy anger, but Sharlotta wasn't sure whether the anger was for Orgun — or for them.

Little Johja, who had stopped crying and was staring at Blue Moon with a curious fascination, went up to her and, staring as if for all the world she wanted to console her, put out her small hand and touched the Korgan girl, whose anger seemed suddenly to melt away as she stared back at the tiny Creel.

It was then that Sharlotta heard her name shouted in the distance.

"That be Petey!" she said, peering in the direction of the shout. It wasn't clear exactly where the shout had come from, and she looked about in confusion.

"It was from there," Blue Moon said, pointing toward a distant yellow gleam against a curtain of black smoke: a golden X of crossed lightning bolts, notorious symbol of the loathed enemy.

Sharlotta looked at Blue Moon dubiously — could she trust her? What if she was sending them into a trap? After all, she was sending them toward the center of the fire — but then, what alternatives did they have?

Muttering an uncertain "Thanked be you" to the Krogan girl, she grabbed her siblings and started running toward the distant gleam. She glanced back and saw Blue Moon, who was watching them a little sadly, vanish in a swirl of smoke.

The three children were running against the current of rushing Korgans, so their progress was slow. Sometimes they lost sight of the golden X. Then it would pop up above the tents again, sometimes closer, sometimes farther away, and they would have to turn back toward it again and struggle on. At one point Sharlotta picked up little Johja and let her ride on her back.

Then she heard Petey shouting her name again, this time not far away.

"Come on!" Sharlotta cried out encouragingly as Beely was starting to blubber and Johja was hugging her neck fit to choke her. "We be there, almost."

And, heedlessly, she ran straight through a troop of Korgan soldiers running toward them.

"Watch it!" the Korgans shouted as the soldiers parted for them. A short, stubby Korgan glared at them.

Then they turned into an open space, and Sharlotta saw the crossed lightning bolts standing against the sky above the priest's moving altar, and she turned away in disgust. She slipped, pulling her siblings behind her, under a kind of food truck (it looked like) parked nearby, hunkered down behind one of the wheels and peered outside.

Chapter 12

Caught!

Petey had been shouting his head off for fifteen minutes; they should have heard him by now, they hadn't been that far away. And he shouldn't be drawing attention to himself by shouting a non-Korgan name even in the middle of the mayhem. The memory of the torture chamber made him want to avoid capture at all costs: the torture instruments had been lined up in the dismal cell in a row of increasing terror — One Eye had only just begun his monstrous work on Sharlotta's poor father, and look what a wreck the Korgan had made of him. Sharlotta had better bring her brother and sister here soon, or he'd have to go looking for them.

Then he heard a pair of little feet running up on the other side of the altar. It was about time!

The feet stopped, then a small figure dunked under the apron, and Petey's voice, about to call out, stuck in his throat.

It was Bang Bang.

There were half a dozen wooden rollers in the dimly lit space under the moving altar, and Petey snuck behind the closest one, between him and the apron, not realizing that this caused a prominent bulge in the drape outside.

"Paona!" Bang Bang called out. "In here I know you be — I hear you shouting. Who but Paona would a funny name have like Sharrr-lut-tuh!"

Petey froze.

Then he heard a strange voice behind him.

"What be this?"

A hand pulled up the drape, grabbed Petey by the belt, and dragged him outside. Another hand grabbed him by the back of his shirt and yanked him off the ground, and Petey dangled there, about a foot from the ground, facing a short, stocky Korgan soldier in a rumpled uniform and with a scar across his face, which was an inch or two from Petey's own face, glowering at him.

"What're be you doin' under Altar of Ramora, you little — why, you not look . . ." the ugly Korgan was saying as Bang Bang scrambled out into the open.

"Be he a Paona spy!" Bang Bang shouted. Then he added, on an inspiration: "He start the fire!"

Of course Bang Bang had not seen Petey light the black tent with his match, nor had he seen Petey set the trash fire to distract the guards before that — he was just guessing. But Petey realized how plausible it all sounded, and his shirt collar was choking him too hard for him to deny or protest with anything but an inarticulate gagging sound.

"Gaggh!" he protested. "Gaggh!"

"What he be saying?" said the short Korgan.

"How should I know?" said Bang Bang. "I don't know Paona!"

Then he moved in for the coup de grace.

"But prove it I can!" And he jumped up and snatched Petey's cap off his head, uncovering Petey's blaze of orange hair.

"Gaggh!" Petey protested even more loudly.

The Korgan needed no further proof.

"We with Paona *liars* and *fire* lovers know what to do! We them a little of their own medicine give! We let them on their own *fire lie*! Hey, orangehead! How like you that?""

"That be right!" shouted Bang Bang, not quite getting the pun but laughing to pretend he did. "That be right!"

And the soldier jerked Petey by his shirt and started off toward where the fire was raging across the camp.

Bang Bang ran after them, taunting Petey as he swung like a pendulum from Scarface's raised fist.

Sharlotta had watched the whole scene from

under the food truck, which, unattended, had supplied the three of them with a dozen stale doughnuts without holes for a belated breakfast, as they were all famished.

She watched helplessly as Petey was marched off. She so wanted to follow them, but she also had to think of her siblings. It was bad enough to have to abandon her parents till they found an escape route, but she couldn't abandon Beely and little Johja, however briefly, on what might well be a hopeless mission to rescue Petey — and if possible, pay back Bang Bang. On the other hand, she owed Petey — they all did. And she liked her new friend — he had proven he was a friend — from Howtiz. If only his hair weren't so orange!

She could not just let them hand Petey over to be tortured or worse (she hadn't heard the Korgan's terrible words but knew he meant Petey no good). She had to take a chance.

"You see them take our friend Petey away?" Sharlotta said, pointing toward the stubby Korgan and Bang Bang and Petey, who hung by the scruff of his neck, like a cat, from the Korgan's outstretched arm as they moved off.

The little ones nodded somberly.

"Well," said Sharlotta, in her most grown-up voice, "we must to rescue our friend. And you must promise be very quiet and not make sound, because if you do, we again might be caught, and you know what happen then!"

Remembering what had happened to his father, Beely whimpered and little Johja blinked hard, twice.

"Not whimper!" Sharlotta commanded. "That be just what I mean! We must be quiet absolute."

And Beely stopped, in mid-whimper, cleared his little throat and became quiet.

"We must to make no sound, until I say so!" Sharlotta went on. "So — you promise?"

Beely squeezed his lips shut in what looked like a tightly squeezed upside down horseshoe, and stopped breathing.

"You can breathe, Beely — just not make sound!"

Little Johja looked at Beely and then at Sharlotta and blinked hard, and then nodded in solemn silence.

"Breed!" she said. "No sound!"

"Keep close to me now," Sharlotta said, and they snuck out from under the food truck and went after the departing trio, who she could just see disappearing into the smoke.

Unbeknownst to them, a small shadow appeared from behind a donkey tied up not far from the food cart, and quietly flitted after them.

"Haugh!" went the donkey.

"Oh!" said the shadow, turning back and impatiently untying the donkey, which fled away from the smoke. Then the shadow ran after Sharlotta and the little ones just as they vanished around a corner.

Chapter 13

The Shed

"We a little arsonist have got!" the Korgan cried out as he marched Petey through the camp. "We the little Paona firebug got!"

Korgans stopped along the way and shouted angrily, "What? Who?"

"We who started the fire got!" the stumpy Korgan shouted back.

"You him got?"

"We him got! Here he be! We him shall in his own fire burn!"

And they were soon surrounded by angry Korgans marching with them in a small ragged, whooping crowd toward the fire.

"The arsonist burn! The Paona burn! Burn him! Burn him! Burn him!"

The soldier, though he was short, held Petey above his head high as he could stretch, where the boy swung helplessly, petrified with terror above an angry sea of Korgan faces, fingers pointing and fists shaking at him. Some of those near him pinched and slapped him. All taunted and harassed the helpless boy.

One of the bigger Korgan soldiers suddenly grabbed Petey and lifted him up even higher, so all could see the malefactor. Petey felt himself starting to cry as he was lurched high in the air.

"The Paona burn! Burn him now!"

Sharlotta, who, with her siblings, was following just beyond the fringe of the crowd, had, in a panic, for a moment lost sight of Petey, but now she could see him again, stiff with fear, lifted in the big Korgan's hand above the heads of the mob.

"Burn him! Burn him! Burn him!" the crowd chanted. "To the fire! To the fire!"

And they hurtled in a wave toward the conflagration that was eating its way across the camp like a rising tide, carrying Petey to it like a criminal or a sacrifice.

As the crowd approached the fire through shrouds of smoke, they suddenly halted and parted, and Petey, half fainting from fear and smoke and the heat, blurrily saw a figure he dimly recognized, dark against the flames, come up to the Korgan who was holding him.

"Bring the little imp with me," the figure, who was covered with ashes, his clothes torn and burned, ordered gruffly. "He be not alone. Our little firebug help the captives free. And you know where they now be. Don't you!"

The figure grabbed Petey's forelock and

wrenched his face up until the boy found himself staring, teary eyed, into the face of One Eye.

"No, sir," Petey whimpered, honestly enough. Right now he felt like he knew absolutely nothing whatsoever.

"We see about that," said One Eye. And he slapped Petey's head down with contempt.

"Go!" One Eye shouted at the rest of the crowd. "Help the camp save, or go save yourselves!"

And the crowd, shaking their fists at Petey one last time, reluctantly dispersed. They had missed their chance for a little entertaining revenge, seeing the little arsonist fry in his own fire.

"We have work to do," said One Eye to the two soldiers and eyeing the fire defiantly. "While still we can."

Then he stalked away, the two soldiers, the tall one and the stubby one, following with Petey. They marched him to an ominous-looking shed far off from the fire and tossed him inside.

The silence within the dim, foul-smelling shed was profound. There was only one small window, high in the wall and covered with a film of dirt and cobwebs. They might have been a thousand miles away from the mayhem roiling the camp. One Eye clearly had only one thing presently on his mind.

"Now, you imp," he said to Petey. "We need to have a talk."

One Eye suddenly grinned genially, looking Petey over from where he towered above him.

"I say that be quite clever. You almost look like Korgan kid. I thought all of you Paona hate dirt, but you be practically bathed in mud . . ."

"I'm not a Paona!" Petey blurted out.

The Korgan stared coldly at him.

"You do look strange for one, or any of their . . . 'friends.' Wrong ears. Wrong skin. Wrong voice. Above all: wrong hair! What be you, then?"

Petey was a bit startled by the question. He had never asked himself that. He thought for a hard moment. What, in fact, was he?

"*Well*?" the Korgan demanded.

"I'm a little boy!" Petey said, defiantly. "I'm a person!"

The Korgan's eye screwed into a red scowl.

"A little boy! A person!" he said, with disbelief and disgust, as if Petey had claimed he was a wobbly gnat or the prince of the stars. "Where be you from?"

Petey remembered something Sharlotta had said, then said, speaking carefully, "I'm from Howtiz."

One Eye's face went slack for a moment. His expression was inscrutable.

"You be a little boy from Howtiz, be you? Well, I think you be a little firebug liar! I be a Korgan

— and *this* is *how* it is!" And he slapped Petey as hard as he could across the face.

Petey's head snapped back and he saw stars — in different colors, in broad daylight. He had tried to answer the questions as honestly as he knew how — and he was being accused of lying? Petey had never been very good at lying — his parents had always said he was transparent. And now he was being punished for telling the truth? He was shocked and frightened. What could he say that One Eye would believe was true?

"Now, who be you, and where from you be?"

"My name is Petey Myshkin Stephenson, and I come from the town of Halloway. It's in" and he named the state.

"Never heard of it! How you get here?"

"A yellow trolley," Petey muttered, anticipating another slap.

"What? Speak up!"

"A yellow trolley . . . to Otherwise," Petey said, lowering his head.

"And how long you been in — Otherwise?"

"Since this morning." Right now it felt to Petey like a year at least.

"This morning! So you be in it before we blow it up?"

One Eye was silent for a moment.

"Yes," said Petey in a small voice.

As Petey's head was still bent in submission, all he could see of One Eye was his muddy boots; they looked just like the boots he had seen in the grass this morning, except they were now also smeared with ashes as well as mud, and streaks of red he did not want to think too hard about.

"You be dangerous than I know," the other said, almost to himself. "Or you be more valuable."

There was a shriek outside the door, and the two Korgan guards entered, dragging in Sharlotta, Beely and little Johja. Sharlotta was raging, in full combat against Big Boy (as, in his mind, Petey called the tall Korgan), who was carrying her, and Beely was pop-eyed with wonder and little Johja wailing in the arms of Scarface, who Sharlotta gave a vigorous kick to whenever he got too close.

"These Paonas be sneaking around the shed," said Big Boy.

One Eye gave the new captives a frosty look, recognizing the little ones from his interrogation session with their father that morning. Then he grinned. This was turning out better than he could have conceivably hoped. Wherever the chicks were, the hen, and her wounded rooster, could not be far behind.

He gestured to a corner. "*There put.*"

The guards tossed the three children into the corner and left.

"Let us be out of here, you . . ." Sharlotta shouted at the top of her lungs: "*bully!*"

"If you wish me your little Howtiz friend here to kill," One Eye said in a quiet voice, gently swinging Petey up off the ground like a pendulum, "you will keep it up please."

Sharlotta went silent but did not switch off her glare.

"All now we must do is for the parents wait," said One Eye, coolly. "They cannot very far have gone after what I to your daddy did."

At this Sharlotta went red with rage, but kept quiet.

One Eye — or Orgun Ramora of Ramora, as Sharlotta knew his name to be — stared thoughtfully at Petey, who the Korgan had dropped into the opposite corner, and stood for a long moment, towering above him.

"You know, young man," One Eye said at last, his voice suddenly soft. "You and I do not have enemies to be. In fact, you do not these Paonas anything owe. Look upon them — " And he turned and gestured toward the trio — "shivering like animals, cold and hungry, helpless and weak. All they do is you into trouble get. One nasty thing after another! And now you accused of starting the fire be. What have they given you? Trouble. What can they do for you? Nothing. Now even your life be at risk. And why? Because of them. It would have been better if you had never them met. It a pity be. Nothing whatsoever can them now save. But" — And his voice became even softer. — "you saved can be. "You and I friends can be. I protect you can, and you get out of this . . . this mess. I the crowd outside convince can that you have nothing to do with fire. They to me will listen. You this understand? You this believe, do you not?""

He waited. Petey gloomily nodded where he stood unsteadily on the dirt floor.

"All you need do," One Eye went on, "is one thing to me tell."

The boy, silent and suspicious, stared up at the powerful Korgan. He felt a tug of anticipation. And he also felt remorse, as if he had already, in his heart, betrayed his friends.

"If you me tell just exactly where the yellow trolley to Otherwise did enter."

"Well," said Peter, with an ill-timed attack of common sense, "if you just follow the tracks where you blew the trolley up, you can find it out for yourself."

One Eye's face went cold and he raised his hand to strike Petey again. Then he seemed to think better of it and lowered his hand. The tracks in the woods disappear, in a tangle of metal and flowers, a cloud of ferns, a fog of shadows. No;

there be no way for anyone to find the way to How-tiz that way. I need *exactly* know where Otherwise *you* enter." One Eye seemed to catch himself, and his voice went soft again: "You can that for me remember, no? Anything at all you remember of the exact moment you here came. That tell me, and as free as a bird you will be. Freer! Birds only can fly. But you be a little boy, a person, and you free will be as the soul — something we Korgans have not, and for which you I envy. Yes, I admit it; for that, you I envy!" One Eye suddenly appeared abject, humble, even pained. He suddenly knelt in front of Petey, so he no longer towered above him but was at the level of Petey's face. "I a secret will you tell, just between us. All in Otherwise no souls have. We be only flesh and bone and meat, energy and matter. We be not real. And we long real to be in the only way we can: by we enter Howtiz. . . . I tell you what," One Eye said, in an intimate voice, looking down at the floor for a moment, then looking up again. He had suddenly looked vulnerable, and Petey almost felt sorry for him. "If you take me to the place where the yellow trolley Otherwise enter, I help you to your home go, back to parents, family, friends. You can all of this behind you leave. No more nasty Korgans, no more big, ugly one-eyed jailer. No more fear. You can that all this ever happened forget, as if it be no more than bad dream. And you home can go. . ." The Korgan stopped, paused to consider; then suddenly said, as though just thinking of this, and as if it were the greatest gift he could possibly offer: "One thing more. Not only you will free be. Your friends here too free will be." He gestured toward the three frightened children huddled in the opposite corner. "You, all be free."

Sharlotta, straining her ears, could hear most of this despite the intense quietness with which Orgun Ramora had spoken, and, her mind whirring at an astonishing pace, she suddenly realized the implications: if the Korgan discovered where the yellow trolley had entered Otherwise, not only was Otherwise in danger of being lost, but the world that Otherwise depended on to exist at all — the world of Howtiz — would finally, after generations of conflict and centuries of struggle, be vulnerable to conquest by the Korgans. Everything would be frozen, entombed, forever in Is. And there would be no Otherwise again.

"Petey! He lie! He never let you free! He never let us free! Not tell! Never tell . . . !"

"*Shut, Paona, up!*"

Petey froze, terrified and guilty. He had been on the verge of telling what he remembered seeing as the yellow trolley had entered Otherwise — the old covered bridge in the woods not far from the field of battle — the prospect of escaping back home from Otherwise was the greatest temptation he had ever felt. But a little voice in the back of his mind told him, if he did, he would never escape Otherwise alive.

One Eye, infuriated by the girl's outburst, slipped off his belt and approached her.

At that moment there was the sound of stone hitting the dirty window.

This was followed by a shout, in a strange, froggy, childlike treble, "Orgun Ramora! To face me I you dare!"

The Korgan stopped and crept up to the side of the glass, flattening himself against the wall, and peered carefully out. His face froze as he seemed to recognize the person outside. He looked down and to the side.

"Little one . . ." he muttered under his breath.

Suddenly he glanced to the other side of the window, but too late. A mirror lying in the dirt outside the hut was laughing at him. But the danger was not coming from there, it was from the exactly opposite direction . . .

A burst shattered the window and One Eye reeled back into the room, glass shards sticking from his face — a missile had broken the window, piercing his eye — and, shouting in pain, he stumbled blindly around the room.

A moment later, the face of Blue Moon appeared in the window and she fumbled it open and slipped inside, pressing her finger to her lips so none of the others would give her away. A little sling shot lay over her shoulder. Blue Moon lightly ran to the corner farthest from the broken window and shouted to get One Eye's attention, while pointing from the others to the open window.

"I frightened! I scared!" Blue Moon cried out in false, high tones. "Oh! oh!"

"*You!*" roared Orgun Ramora.

He lunged at Blue Moon, rocking from side to side unsteadily on his legs. She slithered between his knees and ran to the corner away from the window, and squealed. He lunged after her.

As this crazed dance of the Korgans — one big, blinded, in pain, the other small, alert and making shrill, squealing noises — went on in the shed, the four other children, as quietly as they could (the two little ones had been terrified into silence), crept to the window and crawled out, Petey first with help from Sharlotta, then the two little ones, then Sharlotta herself, as Blue Moon taunted and distracted the raging, sightless Korgan, like Odysseus the Cyclops in the ancient epic.

Sharlotta looked back one last time before slipping to the ground, just as Blue Moon, with a shard of glass in her hand (it seemed to be bleeding), struggled with One Eye, and just as, as bad luck would have it, he reached out at random and grabbed her by the neck, and squeezed with a surprised cry, "I you have, little one!"

"Sharlotta!" Petey shouted, and she leapt to the ground, not knowing what happened next inside the shed.

Chapter 14

Conflagration

The fire had spread like an angry flood while they were trapped in the shed. It was now a tempest of flames, the sky above it darkening into a forest-green twilight. The guards had escaped. A gale of scorching wind tore through the camp, picking the children up and pushing them over the ground as though they were no more than rag dolls. Flames shot above them high as church spires. The fire was like a living thing grabbing, devouring, crushing as it marched through the camp, stepping from tent to shack to barrack. This part of the camp was like a city under siege. The smoke billowed into a towering black cloud that turned half the sky into night.

They stopped and stared at the fire in awe. The intensity of the heat was turning their faces red. Then, seeing a break between two arms of the fire, they made a dash for it, Sharlotta grabbing Beely and little Johja by the hand.

Little Johja stumbled and fell and Sharlotta and the others had to stop.

"Where Mummy?" shouted little Johja. "I

want Mummy!"

"*Crying stop!*" Sharlotta shouted back.

But it wasn't little Johja who was crying. It was Sharlotta, the tears falling uncontrollably down her face. Her sister had only said what she, too, was bursting with inside. And the enormity of the fire made the unthinkable possible.

What if their parents were already dead?

But she mustn't break down now. Now she had to hold on to herself, not let herself go to the emotions going on in full tantrum inside her, or they might never get out of here. She felt as though she were being wrenched in two; she was leaving her childhood behind, it was disappearing down the wells of her little sister's eyes. "Mommy we find! Promise I! *Promise I!* But we no can stay here. To where Mommy is, we must go . . ."

Little Johja stopped wailing and stared up at her sister with a look that said it wanted to believe her but wasn't sure it could. Petey and Beely stood waiting. The younger boy looked like he was waiting to see if Sharlotta had stopped her tears before starting a crying jag of his own. At least that was Petey's thought.

"We'll be burned to a crisp if we don't get going!" he said, truly enough.

Then Sharlotta heard in the distance behind them a small voice crying out.

"Wait! . . . Wait! . . ."

They turned and peered through the smoke blowing in waves between them and the distant shed.

The owner of the voice appeared as abruptly as an apparition out of the smoke.

It was Blue Moon, bruised from her struggle with One Eye and limping on one leg.

"All right you are?" she demanded, in her froggy voice.

They nodded bedraggledly.

"Whatever happened to . . .?" Petey asked.

Blue Moon shook her head impatiently.

Sharlotta, feeling grateful but confused, wanted to ask the Korgan girl why she had rescued them, but there was no time.

"A way out of here I know," said Blue Moon. ""But follow me you must. And move fast we must. The fire the whole camp is burning."

And she dashed off, limping, without waiting for their response.

The four glanced at one another, but there seemed to be no alternative. Blue Moon was unaware of the need to find and rescue the children's parents.

"What for are you waiting!" Blue Moon cried out, looking back at them, then hurrying on.

"But we have to . . . !" Sharlotta was beginning

to call out to Blue Moon when there was a hollow *whoomp*! The four looked behind them to see the shed collapse in a fiery ball.

They instinctively dashed after the Korgan girl as she ran down a row of burning tents toward an iron tower they could make out in the distance.

Korgans roamed about, dazed and frightened; too absorbed in fighting an arm of the fire thrusting deep into the camp and destroying a home tent or some part of the Korgan military machine, or just trying to escape, to even notice the fleeing children.

The children passed the charred remains of tents and shacks, overturned carts and trucks, even something that looked like a tank, gutted from the fire and with its gun askew, looking surprised.

Lying abandoned along the roads were dead draft animals — an armadillo-like creature the size of an SUV (Petey thought), and the flattened hippopotamus-like creature with the howitzer on its back, which they had seen before, and a magnificent-looking beast, a sort of camelion, part camel, part lion, probably used for display by generals and kings in parades.

There were swarms of rat-like creatures with two heads, dashing in mobs from commissaries and food depots where they had lived in relative safety, and the children stopped briefly, clinging to each other (except for Blue Moon, who stayed ahead and watched them with impatience) to let them pass, the rats squealing frantically. Every so often, in the distance there was the sound of a massive explosion as another ammunition or fuel dump blew up.

Petey was a little frightened by what his little match had made happen. Though it was helping them escape a fate worse than burning, he promised himself he would never, ever, play with matches, not ever again, no sir, no ma'am, if he ever got out this alive, that is. Not ever! Cross his heart and hope to die if he ever says a lie! Well, ever says a lie again.

Blue Moon pointed toward the iron tower, which they could see through breaks in the blowing smoke.

"A way to escape near here I know!" she shouted.

"But without our parents we not leave!" Sharlotta finally got out. She had been waiting to say this until she was sure they had an escape route.

"Your parents?" Blue Moon asked in astonishment. "But where be they?"

"They be behind a wall in the trash dump," Sharlotta's voice seemed to dip, remorsefully. "Where the fire start." Then she continued, more assertively, "You remember! With your brother you be there, shouting at me two hours ago! We might be then again captured! Did you see what they do to me father?!"

"He not my brother be!" Blue Moon said, petulantly. Her tone was immediately apologetic. "I sorry we nearly get you captured, that before I knew it be Orgun Ramora who after you be." She paused, her eyes veiled with anger. "To stop him I would anything do."

"But we must save me parents," Sharlotta insisted.

Blue Moon considered for a moment.

"All right, to argue there be no time," she said. "I the others to the tower will take, and there we all shall meet. Careful be since the tower be at the edge of the military parade ground and there be and lots of soldiers around there. The trash dump be over there." She gestured toward the east, where a dauntingly high wall of flames loomed, belching smoke across the afternoon sun. "They may not even alive be," she added grimly.

"Not say that!" Sharlotta shouted.

"I'll go with you," Petey said suddenly.

The two girls looked at him, as though only now realizing he was standing there, right next to them.

"Okay," Sharlotta said.

She gave Blue Moon a doubtful look before

kneeling down to Beely and little Johja, who, their faces smeared with a paste of mud and ashes, stared gravely at her.

"I go to get Mummy and Deddy and bring them back here, so you must to go with . . ." She looked up at the girl. "I not know your name. I think of you," she said, ingenuously, "as Blue Moon."

Blue Moon looked at Sharlotta a little shyly, she thought.

"My name is Miua. But you can call me Blue Moon if you want."

"All right." And Sharlotta turned back to her brother and sister. "Follow Miua . . . Blue Moon . . . to that tower," pointing toward it, "and to meet you there I bring Mummy and Deddy."

"Promise you?" demanded Beely, looking at Blue Moon with a deep frown and a suspicious stare.

"Promise I," Sharlotta said solemnly, crossing her heart in the supreme gesture of honor, more powerful in the nation of childhood than a hand on a Bible in adulthood's court.

Little Johja put her fingers into her mouth dubiously, but seemed to know there wasn't much she could do: she had tried bawling once, but it had had no appreciable effect. So maybe silent compliance would make Mummy reappear.

Sharlotta hugged each of them. She might not find their parents, they might be dead, she might not see her siblings again. Fire, she knew, was soulless as the wind, ruthless as a cornered animal, unforgiving as an offended god. She forced her mind to focus on finding her parents and bringing them to the tower and escaping with them all from the camp: nothing else mattered, nothing else existed. Anything after that was a blank.

"Good be. What Auntie Blue Moon say, do."

"She not my auntie!" protested Beely.

"Argue not! Now go."

Blue Moon awkwardly took the little ones by the hand (something she had never done before; her hands were more used to being used as fists) and, when the result was not an instant explosion or a lighting bolt from the sky, the three gave each other abashed looks.

"We be going," said Sharlotta.

"Good luck," said Blue Moon, in her froggiest voice.

And Sharlotta and Petey started running toward the east; the girl looked back only once, to see Blue Moon, with her little limp, carefully leading Beely and little Johja, who was looking back resignedly at her older sister, toward the skeletal silhouette of the tower.

Chapter 15

The Spell

The two ran straight ahead, then around what looked to Petey like a collapsed clam bar surrounded by shattered oyster shells, then zig-zagged through a series of little baby fires, then all the way around a great burning army barracks, all the time slipping like a thread through the last fearful remnants of Korgans still in that part of the encampment, many wandering aimlessly as if in shock: a young Korgan woman stumbled by, crying out the names of her lost children; an old Korgan man with a mustache hobbled on a cane across their path, trying to decide what direction was safe, tears of bewilderment streaming down his face; a young soldier stalked past in an awk-ward marching step, clutching his weapon as though it would have any effect against an enemy as ruthless, cunning and pitiless as fire.

Sharlotta felt twinges of pity for the Korgans as she and Petey ran past them. Yes, they had long been her enemies, and had done her people much harm, and they would kill her instantly if they knew who she was, but, after all, they were subject, just as she was, to suffering and joy; they were vulnerable, living creatures — vulnerable (she suddenly realized) *because* they lived.

But she had no time to consider this just now, so she tucked the thought away in the back of her mind, to brood over once she and her family were safe.

At one point she and Petey met a fork between two lanes; the one on the right narrow and twisting, the one on the left straight and broad. A public clock stood above the fork, still functioning amidst the mayhem. Petey looked up at the clock (he had always been fascinated by clocks of all kinds): its curious face had four hands and was divided into 22 units, rather than the 12 he was used to. Petey peered wonderingly at it, and finally figured out what time it was: 15:73. Which was certainly an odd time for a clock to read.

"Come!" Sharlotta said impatiently. "We no can wait here!"

"But which way should we go?" asked Petey, gaping indecisively between the two paths.

Sharlotta stared at the paths for a moment, then up at the clock, then, despairingly, made a decision and led the way left.

But after a hundred feet of smooth broad lane, it suddenly turned into a warren of dead-ends they were lost in for long minutes before they finally clambered out at the edge of the trash dump. It was barely recognizable, most of it burnt out, charred black and still smoking.

A heavy silence lay across it like a sleeping animal.

Twenty feet away from them, they saw the collapsed wall where they had left Sharlotta's parents.

The children stopped.

Petey was the first to move. He crept up to the wall and slowly peered around it. He glanced back at Sharlotta with a frightened look in his eyes.

"No!" Sharlotta cried out, running up.

There, huddled up at the base of the wall were two bodies, miraculously untouched by the flames. Sharlotta's mother lay on top of her father, as though sheltering him from the smoke and fire.

"No!" Sharlotta cried again, kneeling by them, then throwing herself over them. She buried her face in her mother's shoulder. "She still warm!" She felt for her mother's pulse, then the pulse of her father, whose eyes were still open, staring up toward the green sky. "They still alive ago few minutes. They just died! *They just died!*" the young girl yelled hysterically.

"If only we had taken the other path, we might have gotten here before ... !"

She let out a wail of despair.

Suddenly she stopped. Petey stood near her,

staring at her in a kind of reverence at the intensity of her grief. He felt helpless, wanting to help and not knowing how.

She looked up at him. The girl's tear-stained face held a question in it. And in the question was a hope.

"You see time on the clock?" she asked, in a trembling voice.

"Yes," said Petey. "It said 15:73."

"And you see seconds?"

"No."

"You can guess?" Her face was pleading.

"Um — how about 15:73 — um — 28?"

"You think you guess how far from here the clock exactly be? I mean, *exactly*?"

"No," said Petey, "not *exactly*."

"You might guess?" she asked, even more desperately.

Petey was at a loss, then said the first thing that came to mind.

"A hundred sixty-seven feet and three-and-a-half inches!"

"What are 'feet' and 'inches'?" Sharlotta asked.

Petey gaped at her. How was he going to explain *that*?

"Never mind!" she said, muttering to herself afterward, "Maybe it work." She turned back to Petey. "And direction *exact*?"

Exact this, exact that! Is the girl crazy? Petey thought, irrelevantly. *Well, all girls are crazy.*

He looked behind him with a shrug, in the direction they had come from, and saw the iron tower in the distance. It was as good a guess as any.

"There!" he said, pointing.

"And what you thinking at that moment *exact*?"

"I was thinking," Petey said, bewilderedly, "what a strange time the clock read . . ."

"Okay," said Sharlotta. There was a tone, half of hope, half of despair, in her voice. "Now, that thought think *right now.*"

She grabbed Petey by the hand, closed her eyes, seemed to think hard, then muttered a long string of words under her breath, opened her eyes again, pointed toward the tower, and shouted, "Shantih otherwise *there!*"

And a moment later, Sharlotta and Petey were back at the fork between the two lanes, and the clock face above them read 15:73, and the second hand was just passing 28.

"How did you do that?" cried Petey.

"No time! Quick!" And Sharlotta dashed off into the twisting paths to the right, with Petey right behind her.

The paths immediately turned into a labyrinth, and Sharlotta was for a moment certain this had been a mistake, when without warning the maze opened out into a small, shadowy space, and Sharlotta, to her amazement, saw she was standing behind the far end of the collapsed wall: her parents lay, not a dozen feet away from her, in a faint on the ground.

The children ran up to them, Sharlotta grappling her mother and pulling her off her father, and her father started to cough uncontrollably. Sharlotta violently shook her mother, whose head wobbled groggily.

"Mummy!" Sharlotta shouted. "*Mummy!*"

Her mother moaned, her eyes flickering open. "Sharlotta?"

"You suffocating each other! Just in time we get here. You . . . die! You die!" Sharlotta began crying hysterically.

"Sharlotta, sweetheart. I here, not dead, I . . . be fine . . ."

But all Sharlotta could say was "You die, you die!" as she wept in her mother's arms. Her mother embraced her, kissing her on the head.

"But where be your father?" her mother asked.

The father had stopped coughing and pulled himself up against the wall.

"All right I be, love," he said. "Sharlotta, darling, you all right be?"

But Sharlotta could not stop crying.
Crying (Petey suddenly realized) with joy.

Chapter 16

The Tower

The tower loomed tantalizingly in the distance, the two children leading the way, the two parents hobbling weakly after. They proceeded cautiously. Many of the fires had died away from lack of fuel, and they made their way cautiously through the smoking remains of the camp. The ruins reminded Sharlotta of the wreckage of her home, and a dark wave of hopelessness crossed the young girl like a shadow, but she tried not to think about that now. She tried to keep herself focused on the tower, and on escaping the camp. Today must be rescued for there to be any tomorrow at all. Tomorrow would have to take care of itself. She felt herself growing up, fast and hard.

The smoke around them was slowly dissipating; the main fire had moved elsewhere in the camp, where most of the Korgan soldiers had gone to fight it. Those they passed paid no attention to them; they had far more important things to worry about than a small bedraggled band of escaped, defenseless Paonas or their allies.

Petey tried to get Sharlotta to explain what

had happened at the fork, but she told him to be silent about it within earshot of her parents; she would tell him later, after they escaped. Petey, feeling puzzled, acceded to her request. "But don't forget!" he whispered. "I not forget," Sharlotta whispered back. "Now stop to talk!"

Sharlotta's mother glanced at the two as they bickered, and felt herself smiling through her anxiety and exhaustion. She whispered to her husband as she helped him walk. "I think Sharlotta find her hero."

"The lucky fellow find his, *I* think," her husband smiled painfully back.

It was early evening, the sky a deepening green, like lime Jello (thought Petey) or an enormous emerald (thought Sharlotta). The four had almost reached the tower and rested in the shadows, waiting for the others, at the edge of a parade ground behind an overturned cart near a row of the tanks with the tall, narrow turrets.

They had been looking out, for long minutes, unsuccessfully, for Miua and the two little ones. At the far side of the ground a gang of Korgan soldiers were dragging off debris to create a fire break (the fires still seemed far from this end of the camp).

Then the evening camp lights, on an automatic

clock, turned on, flooding the shadows. The four found themselves at the dead center of a cone of blinding light.

Simultaneously, as they raised their arms to protect their eyes, they heard the distant shout of a young boy.

"Paonas!" came the cry. "Paonas! *Firebugs!*"

It was Bang Bang. Petey was the first to see him at the far side of the parade ground.

There was a pause, then: "*They Orgun Ramora killed!*"

The soldiers, who had ignored Bang Bang at first, looked up.

Bang Bang started running toward the four in a kind of demented fury across the parade ground, then Petey heard an even higher pitched shout coming from the base of the tower less than a hundred feet away. Sharlotta was the first to see Miua Blue Moon, in full battle cry, racing to meet Bang Bang.

"*You be a li-arrr!*" Miua cried. "I *kill Orgun Ramora!*" and within moments she had thrown herself upon him, pulling him to the ground, and they rolled through the dirt like two enraged cats.

The four snuck behind the cart, huddling together out of the light as the two young Korgans gave each other no quarter.

The little ones must be near the tower's base.

Sharlotta peered up at the guard's nest atop the tower. It was empty.

The row of tanks led to a fence near the tower, and, as the two fought, Sharlotta led the rest, dashing, one at a time, with the parents coming last, hobbling slowly. Once at the fence, Petey caught sight of Beely and little Johja hiding behind one of the legs of the tower and gaping at the fight with enthralled fascination.

They all watched as the young Korgans kicked, screamed and clawed at each other under the bright lights. Even the Korgan soldiers had stopped to survey the spectacle. The fight was epic, like a playground brawl to end all playground brawls, as the two rolled and leaped and struck in a whirl of legs and arms, knees and elbows, fingers and teeth, and jabbed and kicked and screeched and pounded, and shouted words at each other so nasty they made even Petey blush.

Sharlotta was worried: if Blue Moon lost the fight, even if Bang Bang didn't find them, how would they escape?

The fence near the tower was like a wall that, tantalizingly, gave a view of freedom outside without showing any way to reach it. There must be a way through it the Korgan girl knew, but it could be anywhere, and there was no time to find it on their own. The parade ground lights didn't go as far as the fence, which was already beginning to darken in shadow. The sun was setting, the hour of the stars would soon be upon them, a deep green dusk was beginning to suffuse the sky.

Bang Bang was getting the better of the fight. Blue Moon had more passion, but Bang Bang was taller and stronger and more ruthless. Eventually, thought Sharlotta with dismay, as she watched them slug it out, shouting and yelling in frustration and rage, he must win.

Then Petey sniffed something.

He looked behind him and gasped.

The fire had snuck up to within a dozen feet of them, quiet as a cat. It was beginning to eat its way along the fence. This wouldn't be any help to them, as the fence was made of iron chain links; where the fence broke, melting in the heat as the flames leapt and gnawed and clawed away at it, the fire stood tauntingly between them and escape. And it was moving swiftly toward them.

The rest were too intent on the fight to notice.

Then, just as Petey was opening his mouth to alert them, he saw it. At first he was certain his eyes were playing tricks on him. His teacher in far away Howtiz (how he longed to be back there now!) had recently been teaching the class about optical illusions, and he thought this must be one of them. A great, vague form seemed to

be shaping itself in front of him in the flames —
a leaping, dancing, shapeshifting form of white
and yellow and the black of the smoke, in fluid
stripes, with great green eyes — like a huge tiger
made of fire, but continually changing its shape,
sometimes vast, sometimes small, sometimes like
a lion, sometimes like a gazelle, sometimes like a
falcon, sometimes like a bear, but always return-
ing to the shape of a tiger — constantly metamor-
phosing, like the flames Petey watched during
winter nights in the chimneypiece at home. And it
seemed to be moving toward them out of the fire.

At first Petey was frightened, and almost cried
out. But the tiger of flames seemed to warn him,
he didn't know how, not to say anything, as it ad-
vanced silently out of the flames.

Then, as it moved toward Petey a step of its
giant, flaming paw, it was gone.

And in its place, moving lightly over the
ground, was a tabby cat — a cat that looked just
like the one Petey had last seen at the black tent,
and that he had first seen when he saved its kitten
from being tossed about cavalierly by the Korgan
children outside the camp.

She stopped, looked up at Petey, slowly
blinked, then turned and dashed along the fence
a dozen yards and slipped out through a crack
Petey would never have seen on his own. Then she

looked back on the other side of the fence, as if to make sure he had seen.

"Hey!" Petey cried out. "I found it!"

"What found?" whispered Sharlotta. "Quiet be . . . !" Then she noticed for the first time the fire moving steadily toward them. Her parents turned to see it too.

"The way out through the fence!" Petey said, pointing, though of course nobody but he could see it clearly from where they stood. "The cat just showed me!"

"What cat?" asked Sharlotta. "What you talk about?"

"Didn't you see it?" Petey asked, impatiently. And the words came tumbling out, somewhat incoherently, "It came out of the fire and it was as big as a tiger but it turned into the tabby cat that was inside the black tent whose kitten we saved from the kids who were throwing it around like a beanbag outside the camp and it's come back and showed me how to escape through the fence!" And Petey ran over to the fence where the cat had escaped and pulled a strip of it back, revealing a gap just big enough to slip through.

Sharlotta turned to her parents, who had heard and seen all of this, though of course without having any idea what tabby cat Petey was talking about, and certainly not having seen a tiger walk out of the fire, though of course all of them now saw the fire. And the open gap in the fence.

"Get Beely and little Johja!" her mother commanded Sharlotta over the sudden roaring of the flames.

"I'll go," Petey volunteered and was off like a shot. He ran, close to the ground, to the leg of the tower, gathered up the little ones, who at first resisted, as they both wanted to see the outcome of the donnybrook that seemed to be reaching its shrieking climax, but he grabbed their hands and, using the magic formula — "I'll take you to Mommy!" — successfully unriveted them from the fascinating spectacle and dragged the pair over to the fence.

The mother held back the strip and all four children slipped through, then the father insisted on holding the fence for his wife, who gave him a quick smile, then managed to scrootch through himself.

Twilight was beginning to gather, and they scurried across a cleared strip of land to the forest edge.

Sharlotta stopped and started back toward the fence.

"Sharlotta!" her mother said in a loud whisper. "What you be doing?"

"Something there be that I must see."

Sharlotta went up close to the fence and peered through. She just had time to see Bang Bang brutally stomp on Blue Moon with all his might. Then Bang Bang gave her a parting kick, said something Sharlotta couldn't hear but must have been terribly insulting, then stalked arrogantly away. Blue Moon lay motionless on the ground.

Sharlotta was stunned. Was Blue Moon — was Miua — dead? This Korgan child who had, for mysterious reasons, saved them, fought her father's torturer, Orgun Ramora, maybe even killed him — for Paonas! For (Sharlotta suddenly gulped) — for her. Was it a mystery she would never solve?

Then she saw a sign of movement in the young girl on the ground — first her arm, then her head, then she slowly pulled herself up.

"Miua!" Sharlotta whispered as loudly as she could.

Miua Blue Moon looked toward her. Thinking that maybe she could see her, Sharlotta waved.

"Me thanks to you," Sharlotta whispered softy.

Miua stopped and gazed toward Sharlotta for a long moment. Then (or so it seemed — it was hard to see in the deepening dusk) she raised her hand in a little wave.

Sharlotta couldn't stay. Her parents were calling her from the woods.

Miua knew they had escaped — that was what mattered now.

Sharlotta ran across the clearing into the forest.

Chapter 17

The Trolley From

They stood at the top of the low rise where they had climbed from the wood above the encampment. The camp spread before them in the deepening twilight, most of it now a vast, smoking ruin, with here and there a few remnants of the conflagration, bursts of yellow and red slowly burning out. In the far distance Petey could see an enormous black smudge across the landscape, but, uncannily, it was moving. And he realized it was crowds of surviving Korgans leaving the camp and moving in a mass toward the mountains.

Sharlotta's father raised his voice to speak, leaning against his wife. "The Korgans of Ramora be defeated," he said. "The Paonas of Steed and their friends be safe." There was a pause before his wife added, quietly, "For now."

"Now we must go to our home," the father said. "And build anew."

"Deddy," Sharlotta said, hesitantly.

"Yes, Sharlee?"

"I know how the fire start . . ."

"Oh?"

And she looked shyly at Petey.

"Yes. Petey . . ."

It was at that moment that Petey, who was standing a little way from the reunited family, heard in the distance three faint rings of a bell coming from down the slope away from the camp.

Petey stared into the gloaming. It couldn't be what he thought it was — but it couldn't *not* be either.

"That's my trolley!" he exclaimed, unbelievingly. "I have to go! I have to get home! Sorry!" He looked pleadingly at the small family, worn and weary after their ordeal. They looked at him sadly, but understandingly. "I can't stay! I have to go! I have to . . . "

And with a wave, he set off at a run down the slope toward the sound, stumbling and falling in the dusk only once, then pulling himself up and dashing ahead.

Sharlotta, after only the slightest hesitation — glancing at her mother, who understood what Sharlotta was feeling and gave her a small, encouraging smile — dashed after him, setting her feet with greater care than the headlong boy, with her family following more slowly after.

Just past a wall of brush, shadowy and bristly in the darkness, and a staid row of hickory-like trees, Petey found, to his amazement, a pair of trolley tracks running through a cutting in the forest, and there coming toward him, not a hundred feet off, was a dirty yellow trolley, clanking and squealing and leaning perilously to the right, its single headlight like a small surprised, brightly lit face.

Soon Sharlotta was beside him, slightly breathless.

"But I thought it was blowed up!" Petey said.

"There be two yellow trolleys between Howtiz and Otherwise: one that come," Sharlotta said, "and one that go."

Above the windshield a row of lit-up block letters read "2 HOWTIZ."

As the trolley came toward them, Petey remembered something.

"You told me you'd say how you did that at the clock . . ."

Sharlotta looked at him quietly before speaking.

"It be what I hear me father tell me mother the night before the Korgans raid our house," she said. "If you know exactly where you be, and exactly what time it be, and exactly what you be thinking when you make the important decision, and when you say the right words in the right way to the right person, you maybe go back and make it happen 'otherwise.' Maybe!"

"So it was the Spell?" said Petey, though he felt just as confused as before.

Sharlotta said nothing.

The trolley clanked noisily up to them and stopped; the doors opened. Petey stood staring at this strange little girl standing in front of him, with the honey brown eyes and the soft, cocoa-colored skin. She reminded him more than ever of the little African American girl in the other fourth grade class who he had such a crush on. But not maybe anymore . . .

"Here," Sharlotta said. In her hand was a little key.

"Thank you," said Petey, not looking at the key. "What is it?"

"It be a key, silly." And she put it into his hand.

Petey stared at it.

"But what is it a key to?" he asked.

"Are you getting in, young man, or not?" said the driver with a humorous smile. "I can't wait all day, now."

Petey got up on the first step and looked back, questioningly.

"What is it to?"

But Sharlotta only stared up at him and slowly and solemnly shook her head.

The doors closed and Petey scampered up and put in his token (hoping it was usable in Otherwise

— apparently it was, since it slid into the fare box without causing any alarms to go off) and, still grasping the key, sat down in the seat across from the driver.

As the trolley moved off, Petey stuck his head out the open window and looked back at the receding family, lit faintly by the trolley's back lights. They were standing beside Sharlotta, who seemed to be talking to them while watching the trolley leave — her father and mother suddenly looked toward Petey and began waving, as if they only now knew how he had helped save all of them, Beely stared round-eyed, and little Johja watched with a look of wondering amazement, and Sharlotta raised her hand and slowly waved, with a sad smile, reaching higher and higher with each wave, as if she wanted to touch the sky.

The mysterious eyes in a small face watched as the trolley rode off through the twilight. The wings fluttered calmly, and another pair of eyes appeared nearby, then another, then another. There was a sound, like a low, quiet "who? who?" that sounded oddly satisfied, as if they already knew the answer. Then their wings fluttered again, and they rose, one, two, three, more, into the gathering night.

Petey, unaware of any of this, watched and watched until Sharlotta and her family vanished in the darkness of the shadows of the forest as the trolley moved away.

"Are you new here, young man?" the driver abruptly asked him. He was a plump, jolly-looking fellow, a bit like a big frog ensconced on the trolley's throne. He smiled easily at Petey. On his shirt was embroidered a name: MR. CUTTLEBACK.

"Yes," Petey replied at last. "I've only been here since this morning."

"So, now you're going home to Howtiz?"

"Yes," said Petey, with a sigh.

"Just as well," said the driver with another chuckle. "Howtiz definitely has its charms. I like to go to Howtiz whenever I need a nice rest. Sometimes just thinking about Otherwise makes me dizzy!"

"What . . ." Petey asked hesitantly, ". . . what really is Otherwise?"

"Ah!" said the driver, with a bit of a frown. "That's a hard nut. Let me think . . ." And the trolley rattled ahead for a time while the driver seemed lost in thought. "Did you ever wonder what would have happened if you had turned left at the corner rather than right when you were taking a walk that time? You might not have met that bully who always makes your life so miserable! Or if you had said anything but what you said to your mother that morning last week? . . ."

"Yep," Petey said with a sigh. "I sure have."

"Well, that's where Otherwise is."

Petey gave him a perplexed look. "Huh?" Though he was immediately ashamed of how dopey that sounded.

"It's the place where all the choices you *didn't* make, you *do*." Which only made Petey look even more perplexed. "Otherwise is where everything that *might* have happened comes true. If you had done your homework rather than played the latest computer game — and got an A rather than a C on the last test of the year! If you had told the truth rather than spun your mother a fairy tale — and gotten off with a heck of a lighter punishment than you did when she found out what really happened. If the wind had blown all those leaves across Mrs. Simpson's porch rather than into Mr. Howard's windshield, startling him and making him drive right into Mrs. Simpson's living room — however small the difference, a whole world would have resulted that would have been, well, Otherwise. There's no one Otherwise, there's lots and lots of them, an infinite number, at least in theory, because more are being created every day, every hour, every moment, with *everything that might have happened*."

Petey, startled, looked around him, half expecting to see new worlds spinning out all around him made up of everything he might have done but hadn't in the last few minutes. What a crazy idea! What a scary idea! What an amazing idea . . . Mr. Cuttleback glanced benevolently at him.

"But not to worry! Howtiz will stay as it always has. Howtiz is the world, Otherwise is the world's dream. Howtiz is what it is. But Otherwise is infinite, just as dreams are. Every time you visit us," he added, "if you care to visit us, that is, you'll find another world that might have been." The driver chuckled. "After all, there's just too much that would be left out if there were only one world. The universe must work out every possibility. That" — And he gave the boy a wry look. — "is the whole point of it."

After what Petey had just been through, he could understand at least something of what the driver meant. What Sharlotta had told him about the clock at the fork in the lane was almost beginning to make sense. Though the driver seemed a little too complacent about the stability of Howtiz: from what he had learned about the Korgans, there was more leakage, and a lot more peril, between the two than the driver seemed to realize. Maybe Howtiz was not so stable after all!

Petey looked down at the key Sharlotta had given him. It was made of bright, new copper, with an oval head and little wavy notches. Even if he didn't know of any locks it could open, it would be an excellent lucky charm. A good replacement for the rather too dangerous matchbook!

He slipped it into his pocket, then turned back in his seat just in time to see the sun, a vast blaze in an emerald-green sky, sink to its resting place in the east. He suddenly felt overwhelmed with fatigue after the turbulent day.

I guess that means this Otherwise happened when the earth bounced left rather than right? No! Because it rained east, not west? No! Because the moon went to New Jersey? No! Because . . .? he thought confusedly as the sound of the trolley's wheels seemed to say, over and over again, "could have been otherwise, could have been otherwise, could have been otherwise, could have been . . ."

"Petey Stephenson! Wake up! We're at school!"

Petey suddenly woke, dazzled by the blazing sun just rising in the east in the early winter morning.

Priscilla Li, the pretty girl in the class across the hall from Petey's, was shaking him roughly by the shoulder. She must have been sitting next to him on the trolley ride to school after getting on while he was asleep.

"Okay," said Petey, trying to smile and yawn at the same time, which he discovered was a difficult thing to do, it seemed to turn his whole face into salt-water taffy, and he pulled himself together, with his lunchbox and his backpack, with his homework inside it, and his smart phone, he had really missed his smartphone — so the trolley hadn't exploded after all!

"Priscilla!" he said, excited, and still groggy from sleep. "You'll never ever believe the dream I just had! I was in a land where everything happens that could never happen and there was a war and there was a big fire and we saved a family and . . ."

He suddenly felt a funny lump in his pocket he didn't recognize. Hey, where were his lucky matches? . . .

He stopped, pulled it out and stared at it.

It was a bright, new key, with an oval head and curvy notches.

"Hurry up, Petey! You better come now!" Priscilla called out sternly through the half-open window. She had scurried outside while he was gaping at the key. "Otherwise you'll be late for school. You don't want to be suspended, do you?"

Suspended! He'd almost forgotten. Now *that* was a possibility he was sure he didn't want to happen, ever. Miss Marigold would never believe his story — would she?

He saw her towering over him with her

terrifying glare.

"'Howtiz'? 'Otherwise'? I'll show you *how it is*, Petey Myshkin Stephenson, and there'll be no *otherwise* about it!"

The little boy, never having felt so young or so vulnerable in all his life, hastily slipped the mysterious key back into his pocket, then jumped from his seat and scrambled in a panic out of the yellow trolley.

"Promise you'll tell me your dream," Priscilla called out as they passed through the entrance.

"Okay!" said Petey, "I promise!" And he ran as fast as he could down the hall to class.

Though maybe it hadn't been a dream after all.

(To be continued)

— In memory of Keiko, who loved fantasy in both fiction and life

A Review by **YOU**
would be most appreciated.

Online bookstores often provide a way of
reviewing their books. If you would like to, go to your
favorite online bookstore and write a review.

OTHER *Caveat Lector* BOOKS

BY ROBERT BALMANNO
The Blessings of Gaia: September Snow
The Blessings of Gaia: Runes of Iona
The Blessings of Gaia: Embers of the Earth
The Blessings of Gaia: Auger's Touchstone

BY JEANNIE BARROGA
Turn Right at the Water Buffalo

BY CHRISTOPHER BERNARD
A Spy in the Ruins
Voyage to a Phantom City
Meditations on Love and Catastrophe
at The Liars' Cafe
Chien Lunatique
The Socialist's Garden of Verses

BY MARK GELADE
Navigating by Stars

BY HO LIN
China Girl

Printed in the USA
CPSIA information can be obtained
at www.ICGtesting.com
LVHW041954171023
761387LV00004B/21